FIREFLY NIGHTS

The Vineyard Sunset Series Book Two

KATIE WINTERS

CHAPTER 1

LIFE AS A PASTRY CHEF WAS ALL ABOUT PATIENCE. CHRISTINE had always heard this from her various pastry chef mentors, usually in some ridiculous French accent--and especially back in the '90s, when Christine had been an up-and-coming star in the New York City pastry scene.

She had been a woman from the crumpled ruins of a far-away island; but soon, she'd found herself on her way to Paris, to London, to Rome, and finally here, to Chez Frank, the Upper West Side restaurant she'd worked at for the previous several years. She was forty-one years old and on the brink of yet another collapse. She should have been used to them by now.

Christine gripped the top of the oven and squatted to peer through the little window. The tiny pink macarons, a truly difficult French delicacy, crested beneath the burning light: forming that crispy, eggshell-like top. She'd made countless macarons throughout her pastry chef career--but they always came with a catch. It always seemed that if she blinked too long or thought about something else for even a moment, the eggshell crunch gave way to hard-as-plastic tops--a consistency that couldn't possibly grace the plates of some of the high-rolling guests of Chez Frank.

Frank appeared in the doorway of the kitchen. He wore a remarkable suit, one they had picked out together on a recent trip to Paris, and his cheeks were blotchy, his blue eyes bright. Christine turned her head so that her dark, chestnut hair draped across her back. From down on the floor, she locked eyes with Frank, her beloved, the man who'd ruined their restaurant and the future she had so craved with him.

"They're almost ready," she told him, a bit breathlessly.

"Everyone's a bit too drunk to know they're late," Frank said.

"I'm a bit too drunk to bake them," she admitted. "They'll need to cool for a while. Perhaps it was all a mistake."

"Nothing Christine Sheridan has ever baked in her life has been a mistake," Frank said. He placed his scotch glass on the counter and took another step toward her.

She rose so that her slim frame curled against his body. All the fights had already been wrought--her demands about why he'd wasted their money, why he'd run the restaurant into the ground. They'd had such a remarkable thing going. They had been written up in every New York newspaper; every Manhattan socialite had whispered the name: Chez Frank.

Now, it was all lost—and the staff, Frank, and Christine were there for a final night to celebrate before her very dream transitioned into a stupid sushi restaurant—one of the ones where you pick the sushi off the moving counters. It chilled Christine to the bone to think about it.

Frank was drunker than Christine had realized. This was sort of the game in the restaurant industry, part of the reason she had fallen into it so heavily--everyone drank and drank and drank since the party never had any real reason to end. Their lives were parties--and they lived to serve others that kind of life. He pressed his scorched lips against hers, and her stomach twisted with revulsion.

When the kiss broke, he peered at her with squinted eyes. "What's up, Christine?"

Christine shrugged. "Nothing."

"Ever since you got back from the island, you've been a little..."

"What?" Christine asked as she tilted her head.

"I don't know. You've seemed like you're somewhere else at all times," he said.

Christine didn't answer. Outside, the ex-waiters and ex-chefs of Chez Frank had begun to call Frank's name. Neither Christine nor Frank had given the explicit details of just how much Frank had messed up and driven them into the ground. Therefore, Frank remained their champion, a guy who would surely land on his feet in the long-run and hire them all back.

Back in the main restaurant, the bright-eyed waiters and cooks lifted their glasses to Frank. One of the general managers, a woman with large breasts and an affinity for very low-cut tops named Darla, stood on a chair and cleared her throat. Christine glanced toward Frank, noting that he ogled the girl. She'd always suspected something had happened between them, although, in the midst of the chaos of owning and operating a restaurant on the Upper West Side, Christine hadn't had time to pin him for it or even blame him. They were all just fast-moving bodies in the most frantic city on earth.

"Frank," Darla said, her voice smooth, "I want to thank you for what you've created here for all of us. It's been a home and a refuge and a..."

"Is she going to list all the different words for home?" Christine muttered.

Frank cast her a dark look, then returned his eyes to Darla.

"We will all miss working here at Chez Frank. We'll miss the remarkable pastries from your beautiful love, Christine, and we'll miss the late-night screaming matches when we're all so messed up and stressed out. Nonetheless, we were a family through all of this. And now, this chapter of our lives is over." Darla placed her thin hand across her chest and sighed. "I don't think I've ever loved another restaurant more. Rest in peace, Chez Frank!"

"Hear, hear!" a pimply waiter cried.

The party continued. Christine poured herself very healthy glasses of wine, the kind of glasses that would have made her older sister Susan arch her brow in judgment. She watched from the drink table as Darla leaned her head a bit closer to Frank. She drew her blonde hair behind her ear as she spoke, her perfect lips bouncing. What did she have to speak so urgently to her ex-boss about?

Then again, if Frank had cheated on her with Darla, why should she be surprised? The great and powerful Susan Sheridan herself had even been cheated on. Her marriage had ended, and she had retreated back to the Vineyard. It was pathetic, wasn't it? Christine had always resolved never to go back there. She had gone out and crafted a whole other world for herself. She and Frank still had their oversized apartment near Central Park. She owned a cat. She had her favorite bodega and her favorite wine shop and her favorite cheese shop, all within walking distance. No, she would never be able to have children, but what did that matter, when she had the entire city at her feet?

Her phone buzzed. She lifted it to catch a text from Lola. Now that the Sheridan sisters had reignited their relationship in the past month, texts were nearly daily--a strange thing to get used to. Christine kind of felt like she had two imaginary friends back in New York with her.

LOLA: How's the party?

CHRISTINE: Frank is wasted. And he's flirting with the general manager pretty hard.

But instead of sending that last part, she deleted it. She didn't want her sisters to know just how pathetic she could be. She would make up a lie later.

That's what the Sheridan sisters were built off of, anyway. Lies. There was no reason they couldn't return to it.

Christine returned to the oven and removed the macarons. She had arrived just in time--a moment longer, and they would have crusted over. Out in the restaurant, people started to bang on the tables excitedly, and the music changed to something a little more upbeat. Christine walked to the little window that looked out across the restaurant. Darla had sidled up against a waiter and now swayed her hips against his. Frank remained close by, watching. Maybe he watched her; maybe he watched everyone. It wasn't clear.

When Christine had left Martha's Vineyard the last week of June, she'd pictured herself returning to Manhattan with a renewed sense of how she wanted her life to go. After all, while on the Vineyard, she and her sisters had learned the truth of their mother's death. Stan Ellis--that strange fisherman who kept to himself--had had an affair with her that had lasted years. When their father hadn't wanted to divorce their mother, their mother had gone off on a boat with Stan. He hadn't kept the lights on while they did who-knows-what on board. Suddenly, a tourist boat had crashed into them--and three people had died, including Anna Sheridan.

But for decades, the Sheridan sisters had thought that their father had been the one driving the boat. They hadn't been able to forgive him, and they hadn't been able to come together as siblings. In fact, if Wes Sheridan hadn't recently been diagnosed with early-onset dementia, something that had dragged Susan back from her criminal lawyer-life in Newark, the Sheridan sisters would have continued to live with the original lie.

"Babe! What's up?" Frank asked suddenly, as he burst through the door--nearly banging into her. "You haven't been out with us for ages."

Christine gave a half-shrug. "I was only watching."

"That's not like you," Frank said. His smile was almost evilly handsome, the kind that twisted Christine's stomach. "Get out here. Let's dance."

Christine stepped back into the crowd. Her head buzzed with drink, and her smile stretched wider as Frank placed his hand on her stomach and brought her against him. Back in the height of Chez Frank, she and Frank had gone dancing a great deal-- normally coming in around 9 p.m. and checking how much money they'd made for the night and then heading out to some of the most exclusive clubs across Manhattan. They'd hob-knobbed with celebrities and with politicians and with billionaires, who sometimes invited them to after-parties on boats or in penthouse apartments.

Now that they were basically flat-broke, what the hell would they do?

Christine glanced across the room and caught sight of Darla's volatile blue eyes. Was she jealous that Christine danced so closely with Frank? Oh, but wasn't Frank her actual boyfriend--hadn't they lived together for over a year? Hadn't they discussed the idea of adoption (only for Frank to veto it, due to the fact that he had a kid already from another relationship)? Still, there was ownership to Darla's eyes, a sense that Christine had overstepped.

Christine had been on the Vineyard for many weeks. It was possible that an affair had happened then, especially given Frank's mental state after Christine had left. But if it had, what did she care? Wasn't her and Frank's relationship all tied up in this stupid restaurant? What on earth would it become, now that it had failed?

The song ended. Christine strutted toward the drink table and sidled up next to two of the old bartenders, who grinned broadly at her.

"Christine, it's good to see you," one of them, whose name was Marcus, said.

She poured herself another glass of wine and clicked it with the scotch he was holding. "It's good to be back, I guess."

"Frank wasn't so sure you would come back," Marcus affirmed. "He said that you returned home? That you grew up on Martha's Vineyard?"

Christine had never told Frank she'd even had the slightest inkling of returning to the Vineyard for good. In fact, she'd hardly allowed herself the thought. Throughout her weeks on the

Vineyard, she and Frank had had many phone discussions--most of them screaming-matches--with Christine drunk and out of her mind with rage at his decisions, the way he had ruined them. Why had she returned again? She had wanted a new start.

"Come on," she said, her voice syrupy sweet. "You know the city is my home."

"Heck, if I had a place on Martha's Vineyard, I'd be there all the time," Marcus said. "It's heaven on earth."

Christine sniffed. "If you had said that to me a few months ago, I might have smacked you across the face."

"But you fell in love with it again, didn't you?" Marcus said.

Christine pondered. She turned and leaned against the side of the table. Her heels felt ominous beneath her, as though she'd suddenly recognized just how tall they made her and just how uneasy she was after so many drinks. Suddenly, Frank stomped to the center of the room and clapped his massive hands. His dark curls shook, and he gave Christine a secret smile.

"I just want to thank all of you for all your hard work over the years," Frank said. "It's been a joy to own Chez Frank. But I want to give a special thank you to my dear love, Christine Sheridan. This place would have found only half of its glory if it weren't for your gorgeous pastries. You brought life and love to each and every day here. We thank you for that."

Everyone lifted their glasses, their eyes on Christine. Christine felt as though her head had been dunked deep underwater. She flashed a bright smile, lifted her glass, and then suddenly turned toward the front door, rushed out into the early-July heat, and vomited across the sidewalk. As the restaurant was located only a few blocks from Central Park, the clientele around the sidewalk were high-society, ritzy—the sort who didn't necessarily like the concept of vomit splattering so close to their shoes. Christine placed a hand over her mouth, clamped her eyes shut, and willed herself anywhere else. A few moments later, she sucked in a deep breath, placed a hand against the wall as she tried to regain her composure.

It all felt like too much. It was an ending without any concept of what was next. Her future looked bleak.

CHAPTER 2

FRANK HAILED A CAB FOR THE TWO OF THEM. AS CHRISTINE slid into the back seat, she used sloppy syllables to say, "I don't know where you're getting the money to pay for this. We're broke, Frank. We should just walk home."

Frank was just as drunk as she was, perhaps more. This was their normal stance this late at night. He wrapped his arm around her shoulders and cuddled her close, seeming to decide not to listen to her. As the tires cut out across the pavement, Christine remembered those perfect macarons, leftover on the countertop, probably next to three empty bottles of wine. Maybe they would be consumed by the last remaining party guests—people who could have just as well eaten fast-food desserts, not something that had taken Christine several hours to concoct, not to mention all those years at culinary school to master.

They reached the apartment building. The doorman, Jeffrey,

stepped out onto the sidewalk and opened the taxi door. His cheeks fell.

"Mr. Bolton. Ms. Sheridan. Are you doing all right this evening?"

The doormen at their apartment building hadn't been necessarily welcoming in the weeks since they had learned Frank and Christine planned to move out. They were failures; there was nothing to be gained from being kind to them.

"Quite all right," Frank said. He stepped out onto the sidewalk and nearly toppled over. His large hand reached back to grip Christine's.

She hobbled out after him, grumbling. "I could have done it without you."

Frank whipped around and snorted. "If you actually think you can walk around on those heels of yours—all forty-one years of you."

Christine's eyes flashed. "So you're saying that I'm too old to be drinking or too old to walk around in heels? What?"

Frank staggered a bit. "That isn't what I meant."

"Because you know I'm not Darla, right?" Christine continued. "I'm not some, late-twenties general manager with bright blonde hair and big tits and—"

"You both really need to get inside," the doorman boomed. He yanked open the door and gestured. "It's against policy to let our residents have any sort of altercation outside."

Christine's cheeks burned. How was it she had forgotten the doorman remained there with them, privy to this painfully idiotic conversation?

"Come on," Frank said. He grabbed her hand again and led her through the door. The doorman pushed the door closed after them. Frank muttered something under his breath about the doorman as he stabbed the elevator button for their floor, number six.

Upstairs, Christine and Frank stepped into the apartment they had shared since the big cash had started to roll in from the restaurant. On the far wall was a large painting of Frank Sr., Frank's long-dead father, whose vision of a Chez Frank had led Frank to open the Upper West Side place. In the painting, Frank Sr. was no more than thirty years old, his blue eyes serious and sure. Sometimes, when Frank was drunk, he felt that his father peered out through that painting, knowing all the ways his son had wronged his memory.

Now, Frank stomped toward the painting, grabbed the edges, and smashed it to the ground. Christine smacked her hands over her lips and quaked. When Frank reared around, he brought his hands out, palms up, and studied them.

"It always comes down to you just deciding that I'm the one to blame in all of this," Frank said steadily.

Christine's nostrils flared. "You were the one who ran the restaurant in the ground."

"We've been over that," Frank boomed. "Again and again. But I'm not talking about that. And neither were you, downstairs."

"It doesn't matter what I said downstairs," Christine said.

"It does! You think I've had some kind of... I don't know. You think that I'm hung up on Darla, but it's not true. Not in the least. For the past several years that I've known you, Christine, you've been hung up on one thing."

"Yeah? And was that one thing the fact that you ruined our restaurant and ran it into the ground?" Christine demanded.

Frank smashed his fist against the antique table, something they had already discussed selling to get another month's rent. It shook.

"Don't make me spell it out for you, Christine," Frank said. He then stomped toward the living area, where they had built up a well-stocked liquor cabinet over the previous years, lined with old-world liquor, scotch from Scotland, ouzo from Greece, and Raki from Turkey.

As he poured himself a scotch, Christine tugged her heels off and walked across the thick rug, which they'd bought from a seller in India. When Frank turned around, he glowered at her from behind his glass.

"I'm not the young and beautiful, lively thing you want to play with anymore. I get that," Christine blurted.

"Christine, you are beautiful. Stunning. Everyone knows it. When I walk in anywhere across Manhattan with you on my arm, I hear whispers from all corners. People can't believe that I get to have you," Frank stated. His eyes looked they were pleading with her to believe him.

"That's such bull—"

"It's not," Frank bellowed with frustration. "But all you can think about, all you know is that you can't have children. You will never have a daughter to call your own. It has been eating you alive the past several years, Christine, and I can't take it anymore. You're always looking at me for reasons for your unhappiness. You want me to have an affair so that you can leave me. But if anything, now that I've run the restaurant into the ground, you have your out. You can hate me as much as you want. You can go off and live the rest of your days just like this."

"It's just like you to take something that's your fault and turn it around on my emotional problems! Talk about gaslighting 101!" Christine cried.

Throughout her entire life, she had always known she was a fighter, apt to scream and quake and blast her opinions, regardless of who was in front of her. Maybe because they were both drinkers, maybe because they'd kept up similar lifestyles over the years, Frank was Christine's match in this respect.

They tore at one another over the next little while. Frank rose and poured drink after drink for them, dipping them deeper into their alcoholic anger. At some point, their conversation found compassion.

"I thought you were the one, Christine," Frank said, on the verge of caving. "I lived recklessly because that's what we did together! We never thought about the day after. We never considered important and rational things."

Christine fell to the floor and placed her chin on the antique coffee table, which they had purchased at an auction in Brooklyn several months before for an obscene amount of cash. She gripped the edge of the coffee table, felt the grains of the wood, and marveled that this little piece of furniture had ever mattered to them at all.

"I don't know why I came back to New York," Christine whispered.

Frank placed his hand across his sweaty forehead and rubbed it. It was the 5th of July, and fireworks rattled out from who-knew-where. Christine had always loved the mania of the city in the middle of the summer, but now, she detested it. She wanted to rush into the waves of the Nantucket Sound and just let herself float.

"You told me you wanted to try again," Frank suddenly said.

"You told me that it didn't matter. That our past didn't have to catch up to us."

"But it's always going to be there," Christine whispered.

At this point, Christine knew she didn't refer to the past she shared with Frank. It had been wonderful, at least for a while, but it had also been a distraction from what Christine actually needed to focus on, which was her inner-self, and her family back on the Vineyard.

"I've just been floating from man to man and job to job for as long as I can remember," she said. She rubbed her eyes. Outside the window, the first light of dawn crept up in flourishes of pink and yellow hues. It had been a long time since she'd stayed up all night. The previous times felt like another life.

They had previously made a habit of it: staying up all night to make love, sleeping until just after three when they had to return to the restaurant and start-up shop again.

Ultimately, Frank collapsed on the couch with his head in Christine's lap. Christine sipped slowly from a glass of wine and watched as the New York morning, crested up and flourished into yet another steaming summer day. Frank, who ordinarily snored, kept quiet, his eyes closed tenderly. As Christine gazed down at him, she felt only a vague memory of once having loved him. Now, that all seemed so distant and long ago.

But if I don't love Frank Bolton, who will I love?

Will I die without knowing what it means to totally and completely love another human?

When Christine had lost one of her ovaries, a surgery that had nearly eliminated her chances of getting pregnant, she had spent much of the following year waking up with tears splattered across her cheeks. She always laughed at herself. She cried over people that didn't exist, rather than all the people who suffered in the world. Wasn't this terribly selfish?

As Frank slept on, she lifted her phone and realized that both Lola and Susan had texted her several more times. Sitting there in an apartment that would soon belong to someone else, she ached for the childhood home there on the Sound. She ached to hear her father's voice again. She wanted to laugh with her sisters on the porch and listen to the creak of the porch swing beneath her.

She had returned to New York with what had seemed like a resolution: to make her previous life enough. But now, she knew that it was merely bones, the skin and guts of it molding out. Frank had to find his own way and she had to find hers.

Christine jabbed Susan's number into her phone. As it rang, Christine marveled at all the resentment she had felt toward Susan over the years. Before their mother's death, Susan had been the goody-two-shoes, the one all the boys had been after non-stop--the one who Mom had loved the most, the one who could make Dad laugh.

Christine had always been the wild child, the middle one—the black sheep of the family.

And then Susan had just left Christine and Lola on the island and never looked back. Christine had thought she would never fully forgive Susan for that, for being so selfish. It had left Lola, Christine and their father, Wesley, in an impossible situation, unable to gaze one another in the eye.

Yet here she was, calling Susan for help again.

"Christine! You're up early," Susan said.

"Actually, I haven't slept yet," Christine replied.

Susan paused. "Is everything all right? How was the party?"

Christine swallowed the lump in her throat. Outside, a terrible car horn blared.

"Do you mind if I come back to the Vineyard? I just can't stay here anymore."

CHAPTER 3

GINGERLY, CHRISTINE DREW HERSELF OUT FROM BENEATH Frank's large, handsome head. Before she rushed off, she made sure he was comfortable, that he had a large pillow beneath him and that the fan air buzzed across his face. She wanted to kiss him goodbye, but it seemed too dramatic—a final kiss to sleeping beauty. Christine wasn't the type to lean into such nostalgia.

Christine walked to the bedroom they had shared. On one side of the room was her bathroom, while the other side held his. After sharing her bathroom with her parents and her two sisters in her younger years and roommates after that, she had loved the luxury of having her own mirror, her own time and space to experiment with skincare and eyeshadow and lipstick colors. Now, she blinked at it in its newfound state of disarray. After all, they'd had to fire the maid due to finances and she hadn't kicked her depressive state after her return from Martha's Vineyard. Trying to pretend to live like a normal person with no issues was a difficult thing, something she had never mastered.

She had always assumed that she would find that ability when she gave birth.

Christine packed as quickly as she could: her makeup bag, her swimsuit, her summer dresses and her sandals and her hiking boots. She loaded up first one suitcase, then another, then heard a vibrant "meow" from the corner, where her cat, Felix, had apparently been conked out throughout her and Frank's bickering.

"Felix!" Christine cried. She dropped to her knees and beckoned to the little orange tabby. He'd been such a relief to her after her surgery about four years before and had traveled with her from shoddy apartment to shoddy apartment, all the way to this Upper Manhattan masterpiece. The cat curled into her arms and then dotted little kisses across her chin with his nose. While Christine had been on the Vineyard, Frank had taken care of him, but there was no way she would leave him this time.

This added a level of permanence to it all.

Christine gathered her suitcases and Felix's cat carrier at the front door. Frank slept on. Her heart beat at a million miles an hour, it seemed like as her eyes swept over the apartment. She had left boyfriends before dramatically, in the middle of the night. It had always been something, so she would just pick up and leave, pretending not to care.

This time, however, she wasn't just leaving Frank. She was leaving New York City, where she had lived for the majority of the past twenty years.

Before she left, she changed into a pair of jeans and a t-shirt and swept a brush through her hair. She added a dab of lipstick and a bit of eyeliner and blinked at herself a final time in the hallway mirror. She was forty-one years old, forty-one years old, and on the brink of yet another shift in her life.

When she reached the foyer downstairs, the doorman hailed her a taxi. She slipped a ten-dollar bill in his hand and said, "Make sure Frank is okay," just as the taxi door slammed between them. The doorman gave her a confused look but nodded through the window as the taxi merged with the traffic.

Christine tried her best to eat up every single sight en route to the train station. The taxi cut past the park, her beautiful Central Park, where she had run herself silly in an attempt to keep her slender girlish frame. She and Frank had eaten several picnics there, drank countless drinks, and gotten into endless fights. She wondered how she would feel about it in a few years when, or if, she ever returned. Would it hold the same sentimental feelings for her?

The journey to Falmouth was a long one. Christine shook with apprehension when she appeared at the ferry port in the bright sunlight. Only now had the hangover caught up to her. Her throat was parched and her mind felt glued to the side of her skull. She scrunched her nose and ordered a ticket and a glass of wine from the ferry stand. As they poured it, the sunlight glittered across the white wine, illuminating it.

The ferry left just after four in the afternoon. She sat with Felix's cat carrier on the chair beside her, while the breeze lifted through her dark hair. As her eyes scanned the glowing water, someone hissed, "That must be her! Meg Ryan!"

"Oh, my God. Yes, she does have a house, doesn't she?" another guest returned.

"She looks good after her divorce," the other said.

Both craned their necks toward the lower deck, where, apparently, Meg Ryan lurked. Christine smirked inwardly. Throughout her life, famous people had made Martha's Vineyard their playground. They owned countless houses and had immaculate parties, some of which, truth be told, she snuck into as a teenager. At the time, getting into something like that had been quite simple for her. Age seventeen, with long legs, wide cautious eyes and dark hair, made it a little easier, of course. Plus, being friends with some of the people who normally staffed those bigger parties had given her a shoe-in. Lola had gone with her to some of the later ones and then gotten into her own madness after Christine had left the Vineyard.

"You should go get a picture," one of the tourists whispered to the other.

"I'm too scared," the other replied.

Christine rolled her eyes and sipped her glass of wine. Inside his little carrier, Felix let out a mighty meow, enough to make a few people near the front of the ferry cackle. One of those people, a dark-blonde guy, turned his head and clicked his eyes toward hers.

Immediately, her heart sank.

It was Zach. Zach Walters.

Her old nemesis from high school, and the current chef at the bistro attached to the Sunrise Cove Inn.

Shoot.

Zach turned back and said something to the people he sat with, then stood and walked toward her. She ducked her eyes back toward the water as quickly as she could, but couldn't help but notice how good he looked. Great, she thought to herself. His dark blonde curls wafted around in the ocean breeze; his blue eyes reflected the water; and he was broad-shouldered and very muscular, definitely not dipping into the cliché of the local chef being overweight.

He stopped right at her line of seats and peered down at her. His eyes felt like lasers. Still, she refused to turn her head. It wasn't like he had ever earned her respect or her friendship or anything that might have captivated her interest at that moment.

Finally, he clucked his tongue and said, "Christine Sheridan? Is that you?"

Christine whipped her head around and flared her nostrils. "We only just saw each other a few weeks ago. I should hope I haven't changed that much in that short amount of time."

Of course, it was possible. She had been through enough since then. Plus, there was the potential issue of her hangover, making her look a little run down something that had crept up on her in recent years, tugging grey shadows beneath her eyes.

"Always so happy to see me," Zach said with a laugh.

"I didn't expect to see anyone on the ferry that I knew," Christine said, arching her brow.

"Yeah? Well, did you expect to see Meg Ryan? Because everyone else on this boat is losing their mind," he said, looking out at the crowd.

Christine gave him a slight chuckle, surprising herself. "After growing up here and then living in the city for so long, I just don't have it in me to care about anything like that."

"Speak for yourself. You'll be jealous when I'm the one with the autograph," Zach said.

Christine rolled her eyes. Zach held her gaze for a second after that. It seemed obvious he wasn't willing to step back to his friends; he wanted a proper conversation.

"Remember when the Kennedys frequented this place?" he finally said. One of his large hands reached up behind his neck, as though he wasn't sure what to do with it.

"Sure," Christine replied. "I heard a story about John Kennedy Jr. Apparently, he flirted with my mom so outrageously in the late '80s that my dad wanted to kick him out of the bistro."

Zach guffawed. "You've got to be kidding."

Christine's heart dipped a little. "Well, my mom was something of a flirt, I guess." That was putting it lightly, although nobody knew the full story. At least, she hoped nobody knew.

Zach sat casually in the line of seats ahead of her and then turned back so that he faced her and the cat carrier. "What brings you back here so soon, then? I figured you had to get back to that restaurant of yours on the Upper West Side. Chez Frank, right?"

Christine had had the sneaking suspicion last time she had seen him that Zach knew all about the restaurant's failing and wanted to rub her nose in the muck. She gave him a stony look and said, "Don't play with me."

Zach's lips fell and he tilted his head slightly. "What are you talking about?"

"You know the restaurant went under. It's been all over the message boards. Bon Appetit even did a write-up about how we lost our shirt—a kind of obituary to Chez Frank."

Zach shook his head, vehemently. "I can tell you this for sure, Christine; I didn't know. I really had no idea at all."

"Then you should have thought before you spoke and considered it," Christine blared.

"All I do every day is keep your dad's bistro afloat. I don't have time to check any message boards," Zach stated.

"You're just the same as you always were back in high school," Christine retorted. "Always so arrogant and brash and willing to throw anyone else under the bus for your own selfish gain. It's disgusting."

Zach's lips formed a round o. "I get it," he muttered slowly.

"Get what?" Christine demanded.

"You're still mad about what happened," he said, looking at her squarely.

Christine smashed her arms across her chest and glowered at him. "I don't even know what you're talking about."

"Yes, you do." Zach's eyes glowed bright blue with the memory. "We had both entered that cooking competition for charity."

Christine wanted to thrust the stupid memory away as quickly as she could.

"And, you must remember what happened before." Again, Zach's eyes seemed to reflect the severity of the sun.

"I don't know if this surprises you, but I left the island over twenty years ago. My memories are like a pool of dust that I can't see through. Whatever high school drama you're bringing up now might as well have happened to someone else," Christine returned.

Zach clucked his tongue. "Right." He then smashed his hand on the back of his chair and turned his head back toward the guys he had sat with before. "Well, Christine, it's been a unique pleasure catching up with you. I hope to run into you soon so you can tell me more about the things you think you're too good to remember."

"I'm not too good for anything," Christine insisted. "It's only that some dumb cooking competition from age sixteen doesn't exactly live up to my idea of something to hang onto."

"So the fact that your clam chowder recipe literally failed less than one day after you dramatically kissed me at the—" Zach began.

Suddenly, Christine popped up from the ferry chair, grabbed her cat carrier, and whipped down the aisle. Her throat felt tight with passion, with anger. When she reached the far end of the ferry, she heard Zach's laughter rollicking through the air. She didn't give him the satisfaction of turning around to acknowledge it.

Ghosts. Monsters. Bad memories. High school mistakes. All these things lurked on Martha's Vineyard, hungry for her ultimate collapse. As usual, it had been incredibly easy for Susan to just slip back into the "big picture" of it all. But Christine? She had been the black sheep, the one who hadn't been after love and had, therefore, ripped herself from one date to another, all of them more monstrous than the previous. And Zach? He had hardly been a blip on her radar. She had been a little tipsy and it had been sunset and what on earth was a sixteen-year-old girl to do, especially one who'd so recently lost her mother? What on earth was a girl like that meant to do except leap into the ether of whatever life could be?

Now, she felt she was paying for all that jumping. She deserved it, probably, too.

CHAPTER 4

When the ferry finally reached Oak Bluffs, there was a bright flurry of activity. An enormous egg-shell blue sky stretched above, with chatting tourists and music stirring out of every corner, restaurant and rooftop terrace below. Christine collected her suitcases as Zach sauntered down the ramp toward the parking lot. He lent her a sneaky smile, then a wink, both of which stirred Christine's stomach.

"Jerk," she muttered under her breath.

"There she is!" The words carried across the salty air and buzzed through her ears. Christine turned quickly to find herself caught up already in Susan's powerful arms; her chin clamped across her shoulder. Susan performed a few little hops and skips before falling back and beaming at her. Her eyebrows quickly shot lower over her eyes and she moaned, "You look so tired, Christine. Have you slept at all?"

"Of course I haven't," Christine returned. She pushed her dark hair behind her left shoulder. "It's been a really, really long day."

Susan had been on the island for only a little longer than a month, in total, but already she seemed like a different creature. Although she was still thin, she didn't look like the depressed criminal lawyer who had just divorced her husband back in Newark. There was a roundness to her cheeks, a pink lightness that seemed to beam out through her skin. Her eyes glowed with excitement and assurance, the way their mother, Anna's, had. Christine poured herself back into her sister's arms and whispered, "I'm sorry. I don't mean to sound like a brat."

"You only sound like a brat a little bit," Susan said with a laugh. "And you deserve it. Act like a brat all you need. My daughter, Amanda, never went through any breakups in high school, and I was always so bummed out. I wanted to sit on the couch with her and eat ice cream and cry over rom-coms."

"You're in luck," Christine said with a laugh. "That's all I want."

Susan grabbed Christine's other suitcase and then dropped to a squat to peer in at Felix. "I didn't know you were bringing a guest!"

"I definitely should have asked. I just couldn't leave him with Frank. He's my baby," Christine explained.

Susan squeezed her wrist. "I get it. He's family."

Scott awaited them in his truck. Yet again, Christine marveled at the weight of seeing Susan's high school lover there in the front seat, his hands extended over the steering wheel and an old Led Zeppelin track buzzing through the speakers. Although Scott had never been Christine's type back in the day, given he was such a goody-two-shoes and, admittedly, head-over-heels in love with her sister. Christine had always appreciated that he was easy on the eyes and now was no different. Time had been good to Scott. That was for sure.

Christine had never told Susan about Scott's devolution after Susan had abandoned the island. She had a few strange, flickering memories of Scott drinking himself through age nineteen to twenty, even longer than that, maybe. It was like she'd become a shadow of his previous self, aching with the fact that Susan hadn't wanted to remain with him. Now, there was no subtle hint of that in his eyes.

"Good to have you back with us, Christine!" He beamed, as Christine slipped into the back seat and Susan arranged herself in the front.

"You know I can't stay away for too long," Christine said. A joke that, admittedly, wasn't so funny at all.

After a strange pause, Susan said, "Well, Lola is back at the house. Scott's son, unfortunately already had to leave, but it was a pleasure to have him around."

"Beautiful," Christine said. She swallowed a lump in her throat. In New York, most of her friends were childless, but here, it seemed everyone had procreated and was overly willing to bring up whatever member of the next generation they had created in everyday conversation.

"He's a good kid," Scott chimed in.

"Where does he live?" Christine asked.

"Boston," Scott explained. "He likes it out here and talked a little bit about living out here for a few months next summer after school gets out. His mom wants nothing to do with the place these days."

Although Christine longed to say something sarcastic to that, her eyes glowed with longing as they drove slowly through Oak Bluffs, in stops and starts, with tourists milling in and out and the clouds performing a little wispy dance on high. She used the manual crank to bring the window down in the back seat and she closed her eyes, again inhaling the simmering salty air that was mixed with the smells of BBQ, boats, sunscreen, the hazy leftover firework scent that would probably remain in the air a few days more. It was all there.

"Lola is cooking BBQ chicken," Susan said as they cut into the driveway at the old house. Even since Christine had left a few weeks before, Scott had made adjustments to the exterior that returned it to its former glory. Even the porch swing on the porch that looked out toward the driveway had been lifted up from its rusty fall and now floated to and fro in the breeze.

"Can Lola cook?" Christine asked as she jumped out of the truck.

"I heard that!" Lola called from inside the house. As the windows and doors were covered in screen doors, everyone could hear everyone else, inside or outside, throughout all of late spring, summer, and even early fall.

"We're actually not sure," Susan said softly, shaking her head. "She seems confident, though."

Christine didn't bother to keep her voice down. "Confidence isn't everything. It's just the way Lola's gone through this life. She's only gotten away with it this long because we let it happen."

Lola appeared in the doorway, then, with a spatula in one hand and a massive old apron, which seemed to have belonged to their mother. She swatted the spatula around in a faux-menacing way and then stretched out a wide, generous smile.

"You're back!" she squealed.

Christine swept across the gravel driveway and stomped up the steps into her younger sister's arms. Although she loved both of her sisters enormously, she had far more memories with Lola in that house, during the years after Susan had left the island. Lola was more entrenched in Christine's psyche.

"You still smell like lavender and honey, despite all this BBQ," Christine said, breaking the hug and blinking into her sister's beautiful eyes.

"What can I say?" Lola said. "I'm just incredible."

"There's that confidence again," Susan said as she snuck in the screen door behind them. Scott followed, carrying Christine's suitcases and the cat carrier.

"Who do we have here?" Lola asked, dropping down to peer into the carrier.

"That's Felix. He's a brand new resident of Martha's Vineyard," Christine said. "He's probably dying in there." She dropped next to Lola and unlatched it. Immediately, the little orange rascal leaped into her arms, digging his face into her armpit.

Christine's heart lurched. His fear of all of this seemed to represent her own.

"Who's there?" Their father called in from the porch that overlooked the Sound.

"Didn't you tell him I was coming?" Christine asked Lola, rising up and sweeping a hand across Felix's soft-as-silk head.

"We did, he just probably—" Lola shrugged, before mouthing, "Forgot."

Wes appeared inside, letting the screen door slam shut behind him. A small bit of BBQ sauce appeared on his upper lip, and his hand was filled with potato chips.

"What have we here?" he asked with a laugh. She could see the laugh lines that played at the corners of his bright blue eyes.

"Hey, Daddy." Christine beamed at her father. She stepped forward and gave him a one-armed hug before tugging a napkin from the stack on the counter. As her maternal instincts weren't entirely full-flung, she kind of blinked at it, unsure if she should be the one to wipe up her father's lip. Finally, she just handed it to him. "You have some sauce on your lips."

"Oh, gosh. Serves me right for getting into the snacks before you girls arrived. Christine, my goodness, I didn't expect you here already! Come out here and tell me. How was the big city?"

Christine made sure to keep Felix inside the house while she joined her father and sisters and Scott on the back porch. Felix snuck his little head up into the window-hole of the door and kept his bright eyes on Christine throughout, but didn't make a sound. After Lola poured Christine her first glass of wine, Christine made an excuse and set up his litter box in the back closet and pet him an extra few times alone, whispering to him that everything would be all right.

When Christine reentered the back porch, Lola's own whisper cut out quickly. The very last bit Christine had caught sounded like, "So don't bring it up, okay? It's gone under. It's over."

Of course. The restaurant.

Their father had to be reminded so as not to mess with Christine's mood.

When Christine sat back at the table, the conversation shifted to the topic of Scott's runaway brother, who'd stolen some $40,000 dollars from the Sunrise Cove Inn over the past year or so, along with a great deal from other hotels, inns and tourist destinations across the island. He had been able to do it through the trust he and his freight company, Frampton Freight, had generated over the years; plus, everyone had always known Scott and Chuck Frampton since they were kids. It was outside the bounds of reason to suspect that anyone would ever steal from anyone else on the island.

But of course, Chuck had proven them wrong.

"We got a ping from a potential credit card," Susan explained, as Lola splayed an enormous tray of glazed BBQ chicken wings across the center of the table. "Up in Maine. But by the time the police officers arrived, there was no sign of him and plus, the old gas station didn't have any kind of video surveillance, so we can't really be sure where he went after that."

"And you haven't heard from him at all?" Christine asked Scott.

Scott shook his head sadly. "No. He must have had a lot of money off the island somewhere, ready for just this kind of thing. It eats me up inside thinking about it. Especially the fact that I had no clue it was happening."

"I've been going through some of his documents to see if he has any kind of safe house elsewhere," Susan continued. "No sign of anything near Maine yet, but..."

"You're such an investigative journalist right now," Lola said. She swept in between Christine and Wes, across from Susan and Scott, and grabbed two chicken wings from the platter. "On the hunt for your criminal mastermind."

"I guess it's true what Amanda always says. I can't take too much time off," Susan said. She rubbed her temples and slumped her shoulders forward.

"Plus, with all the work you're doing at the Inn? You must be exhausted," Lola said. She then glanced back toward Christine and arched her brow. "Scott already sold off Frampton Freights and is working at the Inn full-time."

"That's great," Christine said. Inwardly, she couldn't believe how swiftly it had all happened. It took Christine ages to fall in love, to move in with someone, to feel as though someone mattered enough to keep them. Susan had arrived on the island a month before, and already, she seemed like the Queen.

The chicken was delightful, even for Christine's rather high standards. It was moist, fall-off-the-bone, with just the right tang of BBQ. As she ate, she drank glass after glass of Pinot Grigio and found that her laughter rang louder, faster--even as her fatigue felt like this enormous cavern that opened up inside her.

The night before had been one of the most dramatic of her life and now, there she sat, with her sisters and her father, her cat inside. She would never return to the city and if she did, it certainly wouldn't be anytime soon.

Still, she felt she couldn't go to sleep. Lola and Wes both retired just after 10 o'clock in the evening. Scott drove back to his place, and Susan scrubbed the plates while Christine remained at the little table inside, overlooking the Sound. Felix swept past her ankles, humming a little purr as he went back and forth.

"I think it's good you came back," Susan said as she cut off the water at the sink.

"Hmm. I don't know," Christine said.

"It takes a little while to get used to it, I think, but once you do, the Vineyard fits like a glove," Susan continued. She sat on the other side of the little nook table and poured herself the last few droplets of Pinot Grigio. "This has been a transformational year for all of us. Me, Scott, Dad, Lola... And this house is here for all of us. The Inn is here for all of us. I just hope you know how much you're loved here, and how much we want to help you get through this. Heck, I'm still getting through it all."

"You always make it look like it's the easiest thing in the world," Christine said as her eyes locked with her sister's.

Immediately after, she regretted the words. Susan heaved a sigh.

"If only I could find a way to explain just how little that feels true to me. But I know it's impossible," she said. "In any case, Lola and I made up the single room for you. The one you had after I went away."

"That's your room," Christine said, sputtering a little hint of guilt.

"True. But it was also yours. I don't know what we're going to do about all of us coming back. We'll have to add another wing to the house," Susan said, trying out another laugh.

Still, the sound of her giggle felt strange and sour. She reached forward and gripped Christine's hand over the white tablecloth. "Just let me know if you need anything. You know I want to be here for you in everything—especially after we didn't have one another for so long."

Christine knew, but it felt too difficult to agree. She nodded, albeit only slightly, and then walked toward the staircase. At the entrance, she gripped the railing and said, "Another breakup. Another chapter. I don't know how many more times I can do it."

As she spoke, her words echoed up the staircase and seemed to build a song.

When she turned back, Susan held her medical marijuana pen aloft and gazed at it somberly. Christine arched her brow, sensing that Susan no longer knew she was there. It was one of the stranger things she recognized, her sister's new fascination with weed. She wondered why, but Christine had to accept it along with everything else that was happening.

CHAPTER 5

CHRISTINE SLEPT UNTIL JUST AFTER 5:30 IN THE MORNING. Throughout many eras of her pastry-chef career, she'd had to wake up at the crack of dawn, just as the first flickers of sunlight crested over the horizon line. This hadn't always jived with her affinity for her love of wine. Now, as she lay in Susan's bed in that old bedroom, where she'd frequently snuck boys in and out the window after midnight as a teenager, she listened to the birds chirp brightly as Martha's Vineyard awakened.

A headache that was part of her hangover panged at Christine's temples as she rose. She rubbed them slowly, wincing, but continued to stretch herself up until she stood in only her shorts and tank top. Felix was nowhere to be found, as she had left a crack in the door so he could come and go.

Downstairs, Christine found her father at the breakfast table in front of a large puzzle. A mug of coffee steamed beside him, and a piece of toast awaited him, smeared with chunky peanut butter. He placed the tip of his finger against his chin and tapped at it once, twice, then grabbed a piece of the puzzle and clicked it into place.

"Good one," Christine said. She stepped toward him and analyzed the puzzle, which seemed to be on its way to an image of a bright red barn, a few cows, and a large tractor. "1000 pieces. Are you glutton for punishment?"

Her dad's cheeks burned red as he laughed. "The doctor and Susan are on me to put together puzzles like this. They say it'll help me keep my head straight a little bit longer. Who knows? I was never one for games like this as a kid, even."

"I'm sure it'll help," Christine assured him, trying her best to select the appropriate words. She poured herself a cup of coffee and joined her father across the table, peering at the pieces. After a pause, she grabbed one and latched it onto the back-end of a cow.

"Very good. I probably would have needed another twenty minutes to see that," her dad said.

"Are you helping him? He needs to do it by himself," Susan called, swooping in from upstairs. She clacked an earring into first her right ear, then her left, and grabbed her purse. "I'm going to be late. I'm meant to be at the front desk at six. Natalie is going to kill me."

"Natalie doesn't have the energy to be mad at anyone," Wes said.

"Christine, what will you do today?" Susan asked, drawing the purse over her shoulder. She sounded every bit like the busy, go-getting mother she had probably been the past twenty years.

"Not sure. Maybe a swim? Or a hike?" These were not things that seemed altogether fun to Christine's current addled brain, but she wanted to push herself.

"Fantastic," Susan replied, her grin wide.

Had she smoked something already? Was that why she was so chipper this early in the morning?

Christine grabbed a banana from the fruit bowl and watched her dad put together another few pieces of the puzzle. Just after six-thirty, she headed back upstairs to change into a pair of hiking shorts and a tank top. When she reappeared downstairs, she found Felix on top of the breakfast table, peering at her father with enormous eyes. Wes gazed back. He looked profoundly shocked.

"Christine. I think he's beautiful," he said, sounding entirely genuine.

"Ha. Your grandson." She dropped to the couch to slip on her tennis shoes.

"My beautiful grandson," he said contemplatively, his hand atop Felix's head. "I don't know why it's taken him so long to come home to me. But here he is."

"Lola's still upstairs, right?" Christine asked. Under the surface, the fact was, Wes couldn't be trusted home alone anymore.

"I hear her up there, padding around," her dad returned.

There they were: the light footsteps. Christine nodded to herself and stood, stretched, and said goodbye. The second she found her footing out the door, she yanked her shoulders back and inhaled that fresh summer air. The memory of taxi horns screaming felt far, far away.

She shot down the little path that usually led toward the Sunrise Cove Inn, but soon headed away from it, toward the Joseph Sylvia State Beach, which was two miles of white sandy shore with shallow water on either side. It was a place she hadn't visited in some twenty years, a place where she had frequently walked in the moonlight with whichever lover she'd had that week. The little stretch of beach led from Oak Bluffs to the town of Edgartown, located on the eastern side of the Vineyard.

When she reached the long, thin strip of sand, she tugged off her tennis shoes and walked closer to the waves. She loved the feel of the little pieces of sand slipping through her toes, the grittiness beneath her skin, and then, suddenly, the brush of the water against her big toe. She gazed out at the impossibly blue, where it met the enormity of that iconic Martha's Vineyard sky. Something inside her felt as though it broke in two.

As she stood out there, the water lapping against her feet, she heard her name being called out from behind. At first, she thought maybe she had imagined it. The second time, the "Christine Sheridan! Hey!" forced her to whip around and blink up at her slightly younger cousin, Claire, who stood in running gear and a little white Nike hat. Beside her on either side were her twin girls, both in their own running gear, huffing slightly. All three of them had contagious freckles, which ducked and dotted from their cheeks and over their noses and up to their foreheads.

"Claire! Hey! Hey, girls!" Christine called. She was surprised to feel grateful to see someone she knew. It wasn't like her. She was a city girl, someone normally much happier to walk through the lonely streets of Manhattan without knowing a single soul. She ambled up the beach to join them in the center.

"I had no idea you were coming back!" Claire cried. "We were just at your place for the Fourth of July. There was no mention of it." Her eyes studied Christine's confusedly.

"Well, surprise!" Christine said awkwardly. She forced her smile to widen.

"No, no. It's great. The Sheridan sisters are really back," Claire said. "The girls are trying to whip me into shape again."

"She's always talking about her steps," Abby said with a sigh.

"My baby belly never really went away," Claire said with a shrug.

There it was: another casual mention of the life Christine had so wanted. Claire's eyes snuck down her torso to find Christine's still-flat, teenager-like stomach. Given all the drinking she did, she really had no right to that stomach, but there it was. Thankfully, Claire didn't make any mention of it being "unfair." She wasn't that type of person.

"Why don't you walk with us for a bit?" Claire asked.

Christine agreed. She held her tennis shoes at her side and slipped into step with the other three girls. Gradually, the twins shot up in front of the older cousins. Christine remembered, with a strange thud in her stomach, that over the previous month, she had spent a lot of time drinking around her cousins and other family members. She had heard whispers from them, asking one another if she was all right. Still, there was such acceptance in Claire's eyes. They fell into easy conversation as they walked down the beach. Small talk about New York, about the girls' favorite subjects in school, and about how Claire had always wanted to go to Paris to see all the pristine flower shops, as that was her career.

"By the way, Christine, you work as a pastry chef, don't you?" Claire asked.

"I do. Or did. I don't know," Christine said. "It's been my identity for so long; I'm not sure what else I could be at this point."

"Haha. I get that," Claire said. "Well, regardless, the girls' birthday is coming up next week. We haven't picked out anyone to bake the cake. Is that something I could entice you into doing?"

"Of course! It sounds perfect," Christine replied. She was surprised to feel how much she meant it, too. The girls were adorable, nearly fifteen years old, and she was weightless and unsure, very much in need of a place to put her talents.

"Great. This is fantastic. My husband will be so pleased. Oh, and we're having it at the Sunrise Cove Inn, so it won't be such a hard thing for you to arrange, I guess," Claire said.

Christine laughed. "I remember those times. Having our family all around us all the time for every birthday, every holiday, every single important moment. I think even your dad taught me how to ride a bike for the first time. It's crazy."

"Well, I guess we're still like that," Claire said. She tilted her head and added, "Why don't you come out with me tonight? You must know what day it is."

Christine arched her brow and wracked her mind. Obviously, she knew Martha's Vineyard's summertime calendar like the back of her hand. "It must be the Tisbury Street Fair."

"Exactly! Come with me. Bring Lola and Susan or whoever is around. It's always such a blast. And the girls are too old to pal around with me anymore," Claire said. "Really, it would be such a pleasure to have you there. When was the last time you went to the Tisbury Street Fair?"

Christine had to think hard. It had been so long ago, but she knew right then and there it would do her a world of good to go.

CHAPTER 6

CHRISTINE HADN'T BEEN TO THE TISBURY STREET FAIR SINCE that very last summer before she'd gone away. She had been seventeen years old. Traditionally, the Tisbury Street Fair celebrated the birth of the town of Tisbury, which was even tinier than Oak Bluffs, located just northwest of it. When Christine returned home after her hike to announce her plans to Lola, Lola nearly fell off the picnic table bench and said, "Are you feeling sick? You, Christine Sheridan, want to go to something like that on purpose?"

"Why not?" Christine said. She dropped onto the porch bench across from Lola and poured herself an early afternoon glass of wine. "Claire seems really sweet."

"That's a pretty different tune than you had a few weeks ago when you said Claire had given up on her life and married the wrong guy," Lola said, arching her brow.

Christine glanced out at the water. Just before she drummed

up a response, Stan Ellis's boat snaked across the Sound in front of their place, about a half-mile out. She shuddered, eyeing the boat in the water.

"There he is," she murmured.

"He comes by here almost every day," Lola said, a fire burning behind her eyes. "I want to go out there and throw something at his damn head. I don't think my arm is strong enough."

"Why does he come by here all the time?" Christine asked softly. "Why do you think he would want to see our place? Doesn't it remind him of what he did?"

Lola shrugged. "I could care less about what his feelings are. He is the worst man in the world, in my eyes."

Christine nodded contemplatively, watching Stan's boat disappear around the other side of a rock. She felt unwilling to make any sort of assessment about what Lola had said, given her own history of "messing things up." Of course, she wasn't so willing to forgive Stan—only question the nature of his mind, so long after their mother's death. She clacked her nails across the picnic table and turned her eyes back to her sister. "So, do you think you'll come?"

At 7:30, Christine and Lola met up with Claire at the Tisbury Street Festival. From the parking lot, Christine felt the now-familiar shiver of recollection, up and down her spine. After all, Tisbury brought with it countless memories. Claire latched herself around both of them and squeezed them close. "Charlotte couldn't come, unfortunately, although, I must say, I'm really grateful that I get my cousins all to myself!" she announced, beaming at both of them.

The fair featured a main stage at the center, with plenty of local and not-so-local acts including, when they entered, a very handsome guitar playing man with broad shoulders and a gorgeous, textured voice. As the women approached, Christine's jaw dropped.

"That's not..."

"It is," Claire affirmed. "Zach Walters. He's fantastic. He's performed at several Tisbury's celebrations and other fairs, as well."

Christine's stomach flipped around uncomfortably. Zach's eyes scanned the crowd, thankfully dipping over her, as he sang a song he seemed to have written himself, something about longing, and about growing older.

"I never thought time would take so much time,

But here we are still together, baby,

And I'm still crying," he sang out.

Lola gripped Christine's elbow hard enough to make her jump. Christine grimaced and said, "What?"

"It's your rival! Isn't he so good looking?" Lola whispered.

"Whatever," Christine said, rolling her eyes.

"What was it he did to you again? I seriously can never remember," Lola said.

The song ended then, and the audience burst into applause. Claire whipped around and announced she wanted to buy them all glasses of wine.

"I can't fight with that," Christine said.

Unluckily, after a few more songs, Zach ended his set and sauntered back down from the stage to join what looked like

Claire's husband, Russel, along with some other men Christine remembered from high school. Claire grabbed her hand and said, "Let's go, say hi! I like to flirt with Russel like we don't know each other."

As they approached, Christine stalled a bit, outside the group. Claire tapped her husband on the shoulder and said, "Hey. I couldn't help but notice... you were pretty good looking over here."

Russel poured himself over her in a big bear hug. His eyes scanned the two Sheridan sisters as a smile formed. "Hey, girls! Good to see you. Zach's one of my main buddies from high school. You probably remember that."

Zach's blue eyes beamed toward Christine's. She nodded as a means to tell him she wanted nothing more to do with him. He seemed not to catch the hint. He stepped closer and said, "Christine! Surprised to see you still on the island. You looked like you were on the verge of getting back on the next ferry."

"Maybe it was just you that I wanted to get away from," Christine quipped and feigned a smile.

"Fair enough."

"You're um...not so bad up on stage, though," Christine said.

Why had she said that? Was the wine getting to her head? It didn't matter.

"Thanks. I like performing for these smaller things. Back in Boston, I had a band and it got kind of serious. The pressure was too much for me," he replied.

Why had he just told her so much about his past? Christine arched her brow, willing herself to say how little she actually cared.

"Zach, beautiful as usual," Claire said. She reached over and swatted him on the shoulder. "I brought some guests over to see you perform."

"It's a rare thing to see the Sheridan sisters," Zach affirmed.

"Not so rare these days!" Russel said. "Getting everyone back together again."

They stayed on at the Tisbury Street Fair for the next hour or two, until the moon lifted up like a hot air balloon over the Sound. Christine's head buzzed with wine, and Lola's laugh rang out through the night, with a mind of its own. Finally, after they'd eaten and drank themselves silly, someone--nobody could remember who--suggested they head off to the beach for a late-night swim. Although Christine was annoyed with Zach Walters's continued presence, she couldn't resist it: she loved being at the beach at night.

CHAPTER 7

ALTHOUGH LOLA BEGGED AND PLEADED THAT THEY HEAD TO Moshup Beach, which was renowned for its nudity, Claire convinced Zach to drive them all over to the western point of Aquinnah. Aquinnah was known for its gorgeous clay cliffs, serene wildlife, and picaresque lighthouses but those who grew up on the island also knew it as one of the very earliest places for whaling, hundreds of years ago.

"I can't get caught going to a nude beach, Lola," Claire said with a laugh. "My girls are about to turn fifteen. That would destroy their psyche, learning their parents had been caught there."

"And if we don't get caught?" Russel said with a wink.

Claire smacked him lightly on the shoulder as they all hunkered into Zach's pick-up. After years of city life, it was still strange to Christine that everyone on the island owned their own car. She'd even noticed that Susan had had her car shipped over to the island, after storing it in Falmouth for several weeks. She had fully transitioned.

Once they headed in that direction, Christine said, "I remember once we did make it to Moshup, Lola. Remember?"

Lola, who sat in the back seat directly next to Christine, cast her a funny look. Christine furrowed her brow and said, "What's up? Don't you remember it?"

In front, Zach and Russel's friend, Clark, said, "Oh, she remembers it all right."

"What am I not getting?" Claire asked as she eyed each of them more closely.

Slowly, memory folded over Christine, and her jaw dropped. That's why Clark was so familiar! He had dated Lola for a few months, apparently around the time they'd gone skinny dipping.

"So, that was you!" Christine said with a wry smile.

This time, Lola was the one to deliver a smack across Christine's shoulder. Christine chuckled and said, "You don't remember who I was with, do you? I can't for the life of me even remember what his face looked like."

"It was hard for any of us to keep up, Christine!" Zach called from the driver's seat.

"Hey! Now, that's enough. We're all grown adults now. And oh, my goodness. Will you look at that! We're there! Oh, it's prettier than ever," Claire cried.

They drove past Menemsha Pond and then headed straight out toward the furthest tip, the Aquinnah Cliffs Overlook. There, Zach parked the truck and they clambered out to peer into the darkness and listen to the waves crash down below. Christine walked out further than the rest of them, easing across the red rocks. When she turned back, she saw the five of them in a straight line, all of their eyes wide and big beneath the moon. Only two days before had been her final night in New York. She could hardly remember anyone at Chez Frank. Now it was all a blur as she looked out over the blue ocean.

After the cliffs, they meandered toward the Aquinnah public beach. At night and so far from the traditional places tourists stayed, the beach was completely abandoned and, therefore, a perfect paradise. Lola stripped into her bra and underwear and raced into the waves, with Clark hot on her heels. Russel and Claire joined shortly after. Christine held back, remembering she had worn a stupid thong and lacey bra—nothing as sensible as the others. Plus, she didn't feel as wild and free as Lola did. Not now, anyway. Maybe not ever.

To her surprise, Zach remained on the beach with her, fully clothed. He nodded at her from a few paces away, and she nodded back.

"Not up to swimming?" he asked as he shuffled his feet in the sand below.

"It's going to be cold," she said.

On cue, Lola cried out into the night that it was freezing. Christine and Zach locked eyes for just a split second and laughed. Immediately after, Christine dropped her gaze to the ground. She shifted her weight, wishing she had gone after the others into the crashing waves if only to get out from under Zach's gaze.

"I had no idea you would be here tonight," she said finally.

"Neither did I," Zach replied.

"Oh, I meant at the fair."

"I know what you meant." His eyes sparkled.

"You always have to be the cleverest person in the room, don't you?" Christine said.

"I don't try to be; sometimes, it just comes out. Hey, I have another bottle of wine in the truck—my secret stash. Want me to crack it while the other's swim?"

Christine dragged her tongue across her teeth and considered it.

"I can see it written all over your face. You want to say yes. I'll grab it now."

Zach disappeared for a moment. There was the clunk of the truck door closing, then the shuffle of his shoes across the sand. Suddenly, he unfurled a blanket across the space between them and gestured for her to sit.

"We might as well get comfortable while they freeze to death," he said, letting out a chuckle.

"Ha."

Christine sat and folded her legs as ladylike as she could. Zach cranked the cork out of the bottle and poured them each a glass in little styrofoam cups. As Lola screamed another time near the water, Christine and Zach clinked "glasses" and sipped.

"Oh, my God. This is crazy," Christine said with wide eyes. She grabbed the bottle and turned it to inspect the label. "French. 1977. Are you serious right now?"

Zach chuckled. "I have a pretty hefty wine collection at my place these days. It became a hobby when I moved back to the island."

"This is some of the best stuff we ever had on offer at Chez Frank," Christine continued. "We used to sell this for thirty dollars a glass, sometimes more. And here I am, drinking it out of a styrofoam cup."

"Welcome back home," Zach said. "We live well for what we are."

Christine laughed again. It seemed to rise up out of her without her asking for it. "I drank a lot of this in New York, maybe a little too much. Maybe I'm the reason the whole place went under," Christine said contemplatively, chuckling a little as she stared into her cup. "But hey, you know what? It tastes even better here by the water. I wouldn't want it anywhere else."

"City life ain't for me anymore," Zach affirmed. "All that chaos and noise. When I lived alone in Boston, it felt like I didn't see a single person with a smile on their face for days at a time. It ate me up inside. I felt like I lived in a really lonely world, one with different rules."

Christine inwardly agreed with him. It had been something she had wanted to be stronger than. She had longed to overcome it. Still, she wasn't willing to admit that to Zach Walters.

"Anyway, I hope you stick around a little while," Zach continued. "I'm willing to bet you don't feel the same."

"If you keep letting me drink your fancy wine, I'll never leave," Christine said.

"It'll be expensive, but I think I can manage it for a while," Zach said, flashing her a wide smile.

Christine forced her eyes away from him again. She felt that stab of recognition again, the first feelings of lust. She had to stop them before they became too powerful.

"By the way, Claire mentioned you're baking the cake for the girls' birthday party?" Zach asked.

"Yes. I'm looking forward to it," Christine said. "It's been a long time since I made a cake for someone I actually cared about, rather than a really rich buyer from Manhattan. Think a sweet sixteen birthday party for the second cousin once removed of Bill Gates. Not my beloved cousin's twin girls."

"Ha. It's a completely different feeling. I get that," Zach agreed. "But I wanted to let you know since it's at the Inn anyway, you should use the bistro kitchen to bake it—only if you want to. I mean, it's right there at your disposal, and it would be so much easier. You can even use some of my supplies."

Christine arched her brow. She hadn't envisioned this kind of goodwill from someone she had hated so much. Again, she shoved the thought of any sort of appreciation for him, from his windswept dirty blonde hair to his blue eyes to his broad shoulders (to his incredible guitar playing), into the back crevices of her mind.

This was Zach Walters, for crying out loud. He only did things to get ahead. He only did everything for his own selfish gain.

If there was anything Christine knew, it was that people didn't change. Not really.

"I'll have to think about it," Christine said. "It's a really generous offer. Thank you."

Suddenly, Lola ripped toward them from the water. She grabbed her shirt and covered herself quickly. Her eyes were enormous, her grin so monstrously wide. "We think we saw a whale!" she cried out.

Immediately, Christine shot up and rushed to the edge of the water. Russel, Clark, and Claire all stood in a line, blinking out. Nobody was brave enough to speak, just in case, it scared the whale away.

When nothing reappeared, Christine finally whispered, "Are you sure it was something?"

"Wasn't a trout," Russel said.

"It seemed huge," Claire affirmed. "I haven't seen one in a long time. Years. I would give anything."

After several more minutes of gazing out longingly, the four of them turned back to join Lola and Zach on the sand. Together, they finished the bottle of wine, then returned to the truck to drive back to Oak Bluffs. In the back, Christine listened to the soft hum of everyone's voices, dipping in and out of the conversation, finding harmony and rhythm.

Zach drove back to the Sheridan house first. As he went, he clucked his tongue and said, "I haven't driven anyone to the Sheridan house in twenty plus years, I guess."

Christine's heart thudded at the memory.

"Why did you drive someone home?" Lola asked. "I don't remember you taking me."

But before Zach could answer, she shrugged and struck out of the truck. Everyone hollered their goodbyes, with Christine taking extra care to catch Zach's eye. She couldn't believe he'd mustered the courage to say that in front of everyone else.

Back inside, Lola scampered upstairs to change, while Christine sat with Susan and Aunt Kerry in the living area. Susan looked bleary-eyed and, admittedly, a bit stoned. Christine wondered if Aunt Kerry had seen her smoke it. She guessed not.

"How was the fair, beauty?" Susan asked, patting the cushion beside her on the couch.

"It was actually really fun," Christine said. She huddled next to her sister, who drew a thick blanket over them.

"Susan introduced me to something called a podcast," Aunt Kerry said. "True crime. It's fascinating. You know, they can solve any crime with DNA these days. But it all relates back to that Ancestry dot com stuff. If you gave your blood, and your cousin is a serial killer, he had better watch out."

"All our cousins are your kids, Aunt Kerry. Are you trying to tell us something?" Susan asked as she smiled at her aunt.

Aunt Kerry furrowed her brow. "It's just impossible to ever tell, isn't it?"

"I think you made a huge mistake," Christine whispered to Susan.

Aunt Kerry prepared her things, folding up her crochet and sipping the last of her glass of wine. "I suppose I had better get on home. I'll take your father to that doctor's appointment tomorrow. 10:30."

"Perfect. Yes. I just want to meet with a few vendors tomorrow," Susan said.

Aunt Kerry gripped Susan's shoulder and said, "You look tired, my dear. I think you should get some rest."

When Aunt Kerry disappeared, Christine turned her head and said, "You must be stoned, right? That's all it is."

Susan scrubbed her hands over her eyes. "Yep. Just a little stoned. That's all."

"I knew it. It's the funniest thing in the world," Christine said. "My older, goody-two-shoes sister, smoking pot."

"Whatever. If only Amanda knew. She would laugh along with you," Susan said as she chuckled.

When Lola reappeared in the living room, she did a little kick-spin and landed on her knees, beaming. "Guess who drank wine on the beach alone with Zach Walters this evening?"

"Oh, Lola, you didn't!" Susan cried.

"Nope. I didn't. But his nemesis did," Lola said, wagging her eyebrows and pointing the finger at her older sister.

"What an interesting development," Susan said contemplatively, giving Christine a curious glance.

"I just didn't want to swim in the freezing cold water, is all," Christine said. "You guys are insane. I'm a civilized city girl now."

"A civilized city girl who drinks expensive French wine in styrofoam cups. Got it," Lola said with a wide smirk.

"I would never involve myself with Zach Walters," Christine said. "I've hated him all these years. I would never."

As Christine lay in bed upstairs, she heard the soft hum of her sisters speaking into the night without her. Exhaustion swept over her as she curled beneath the sheets. Suddenly, there was the soft pad of Felix, bouncing up from the floor and winding himself down at the end of the bed.

Over the past twenty-five years of her life, Christine found that these dark and quiet moments were the ones when she thought of her mother most. In New York, she would peer out the window and watch the traffic and consider what her mother might have thought of her life in the city. "So chaotic and loud, Christy, but that's just like you!" Anna Sheridan hadn't fully understood Christine, not like she had understood Susan. At the time of her death, Christine had been fourteen and volatile, on that rocky edge of puberty and eager to spew hateful words and stomp up the steps to her bedroom to play loud music until bedtime. On more than one occasion, she had told her mother that she hated her, something that curdled in her stomach now. She hoped her mother had known this was nothing more than teenage angst.

Still, Christine remembered her mother enough to know how little she would have liked some of her ex-boyfriends. Of Frank, she would have said, "Handsome, sure. I can see why you wanted to date him, Christy. But build a business with him? Live in that big, expensive apartment? He doesn't have it, Christy. He was always going to ruin you. He looks at other people's money like it's his to burn."

"Zach Walters is so handsome, isn't he?" Anna Sheridan had said exactly once, after picking Christine up from soccer practice at age thirteen and taking her privately to get ice cream, which was a rare treat without her sisters. Zach had walked past them post-practice and waved.

"Um, no. He's a jerk," Christine had blurted out.

"He was watching you during your practice," her mother had said.

"Probably because I'm better than he is at soccer. He wants to figure out how to beat me. He never will."

"Oh, Christine. That hard edge to you. It'll take you far in this life," her mother had said. "But I don't know if it will make you happy."

CHAPTER 8

A FEW DAYS LATER, CHRISTINE GATHERED TOGETHER ANNA
Sheridan's old diaries, poured herself a dense glass of Cabernet
Sauvignon, and sat out on the picnic table. Wes was inside,
catching the start of a baseball game on the little TV he'd had for
some fifteen years, and the sound of the crowd and the click of the
baseball against the bat soothed her. They were sounds of a long-
ago life.

The question Christine wanted to ask her mother the most was
why. Why had she taken up the affair? Why hadn't she decided to
work on her marriage and turn inward, rather than leap out for
someone like Stan Ellis, a man who had ultimately been the reason
for her and two other tourists' deaths?

The reason Anna had stepped out of the marriage seemed
inextricably linked to Christine's own mode of operation. All her
life, she had assumed her mother was far more reasonable and
responsible, less brash and egoistic. Now, with her affair coming to

59

the surface, Christine felt she saw something more of herself in her mother.

And she was hungry for more.

November 15, 1992

It seems unfair to write these words whilst my daughters sit in the kitchen together and prepare dinner. Wes remains at the Inn, forever at the Inn, never one to "accidentally" swing home early, or make extra time for his family. That said, I am the one who's stepped outside of all of this, seeking a happiness that Wes has never given or allowed me.

Last evening, Christine was the only one at the house with me. Lola had a sleepover, Susan was yet again with Scott and I sat outside on the porch, all bundled up sipping wine and watching the minutes of my life tick by. Christine moseyed in and out before heading upstairs to read a comic book. (Again, she seems on the edge of some sort of teenage depression, something I must keep up with as she grows older.)

Stan drove his boat to our dock. He's never been so brash before. If I'm honest, the act of it turned me on. I rushed down the little hill and wrapped my arms around him. He twirled me into the boat and kissed me there beneath the lush pink sunset. "My daughter Christine is home!" I told him, genuinely shocked. But he just shrugged and said, "She'll know about us soon enough." He said it with such certainty, as though he's already written the story of our life.

Stan insisted on following me up and drinking a glass of wine on the porch. It was cold, nearly freezing, but he wrapped me in his arms and told me secrets of himself. His ex-wife nearly broke him in two, and he always assumed that he would be alone, that he would never have anyone. I am that someone. I want to give him that hope.

How horrible is it that we become these hopes for people. How horrible is it that once, Wes and I were that hope for one another and we've stepped away from it, exhausted and strung-out from hours at the Inn and with babies and toddlers and now, the reckless angst of teenagers?

There was a footstep on that very same porch. Christine lifted her head to find Susan and Lola swing out through the screen door. Their eyes closed in on the diaries. Christine felt as though she came up from a dream and blinked at them. Lola was the spitting image of Anna at the time of her death and Christine felt overwhelmed with sadness, looking at her now.

"Have you discovered anything new?" Lola asked.

"Not really," Christine said. She brushed aside a tear and tried on a smile. "Although she was having some real problems with me and my... 'depression.'" She put air quotes up, trying to turn it into a joke.

Susan and Lola exchanged glances for enough time to prove that they, too, thought Christine suffered from it. Heck, she did. It wasn't a secret.

"What's the date?" Susan asked.

"November 1992," Christine said. "In this one, you were off with Scott."

"Does she say anything about him?" Susan asked, sitting across from Christine and pouring herself a glass of wine.

"Not really. She always liked him, I think," Christine said. She flipped ahead a bit and found Scott's name again, in December of that year.

Scott is just like Wes in a lot of ways—committed and kind. He wants to build a world with my daughter. I hope she knows what she's getting into, and I hope he doesn't do what Wes did: step as far as he could out of his life while still pretending to perform all his duties as a husband and father. Regardless, I don't think Susan is the type of girl to cheat. It's a funny thing, imagining my three girls as women, my age or older. How will they perceive the world? Will they have gotten off of this silly island? Will they have made anything more of themselves than me, a sloppy, cheating wife?

"Oops," Lola said. "That sounds harsh."

"It goes on to talk about Stan," Christine continued. "Gosh, she loved him. She calls him one of the most fascinating men she's ever met in her life."

Susan balled her hand into a fist and whispered, "How can he be anything but a murderer? I'm sorry, but what he did keeps me up at night. The fact that he's just out there on the Sound all the time, getting away with what he did... I can hardly stand it."

"We should talk to him," Christine said suddenly, surprising herself.

Lola and Susan studied her with stoic faces.

"Don't you think too much time has gone by?" Susan asked.

"I don't know. It's all still so real to us," Christine said. "There's no reason that it isn't still real to him. And maybe we could get the answers we need from him." She paused for a moment, contemplating. "Besides. It's clear that he was the only person really close to Mom during these years when we were teenagers and doing our own thing and Dad gave all his time to the Inn."

"I talked to Claire about him recently, and she said that Stan always drinks at the Edgartown Bar," Susan said. "That tiny one right off Main Street. We've walked past it a million times."

"I would imagine he's a big drinker," Christine said. She drank to duck away from her own all-encompassing emotions and she assumed other people had to do the same to get through.

"He was probably wasted the night Mom died," Lola spat out in annoyance. "I'd like to know that, too, I think. I want to know everything. It's not fair that we have to live in the grey-area of knowing about this, only hearing what Dad is willing to tell us."

"Do you think it would bother Mom, knowing we were going through her things like this?" Susan asked suddenly. "I try to imagine Amanda going through my stuff after I'm dead. It's not like I keep a very good journal or anything, but little lists I make to myself. Little quotes I write down. What would she make of all of it?"

"Don't talk like that," Lola insisted.

"I just think we all keep a lot of secrets from one another, is all," Susan said, quickly picking up her glass and taking a sip.

Christine arched her brow. That seemed way too cryptic for her liking. But before she could say anything, Lola's phone on the table buzzed, making the tops of their wine glasses shimmer.

"Speaking of family, that's my flesh and blood," Lola said. Her face shifted quickly and her eyes sparkled. She lifted the phone to her ear and said, "Audrey! Hello!"

Lola stood from the table, grabbed her wine, and walked slowly down the steps of the porch, her laughter bubbling up through her. Seconds later, though, that laughter halted.

"What do you mean?" Lola said, down below the porch. Her voice was strained, stark.

Susan and Christine made heavy eye contact. It was obvious already; something was wrong.

Susan grabbed a diary and flipped through. Christine saw the date: 1990, probably about a year before their mother had started the affair with Stan. She pretended to read, while Christine watched Lola pace down below the porch. She hadn't said anything in a while.

"Don't cry, honey. It's going to be okay," Lola said, trying to soothe her daughter on the other end of the line.

By her tone, Christine had to guess that everything wasn't going to be okay. Again, Susan gave her a big-eyed, panicked look. Slowly, Lola ambled away from the porch, toward the dock below. For a long time, she sat at the edge, her feet dipping in and out of the water as she spoke with her daughter on the phone.

"What do you think happened?" Christine asked.

"I have no idea," Susan replied. "It doesn't sound very good, though."

"Nineteen-years-old at her first internship in Chicago," Christine said, remembering what Audrey had been up to when she'd seen her niece in the Vineyard a few weeks before. "She has the world at her fingertips."

"But it's easy to think you don't at that age," Susan said. "You're just kind of fumbling around for something to cling onto."

"It was worse for us," Christine said. "We didn't have each other or Mom or Dad. We were just floundering."

"Maybe," Susan said. "I made Richard my rock pretty quickly. Then, there was the first baby and then the second." She clucked her tongue.

Lola reappeared at the base of the porch. All the blood had

drained from her face. She clutched the phone to her chest and blinked up at her sisters, her empty glass of wine, reflecting the last of the sunlight.

Susan ripped up from the porch. "What's wrong? What's up?"

Lola swallowed. In a strange, taut silence, Christine's heart sank. She could never shake the feeling that always, in this life, you were only a few weeks, months, or even seconds from the next big disaster.

"Audrey is pregnant," Lola whispered. She stepped delicately up the porch and reached for the bottle of wine, pouring herself another hefty glass. Her eyes were tinged red. "She's terrified, just living in Chicago by herself, doing this internship. I tried to tell her everything I could about safe sex. I--I--" She collapsed on the picnic table bench and hung her head. "Condoms and birth control, all of it. I told her. I took her to the gynecologist. I wanted everything to be open and honest between us so that she didn't make the same mistake I did. I had her when I was way too young to be a mother. Way, way too young. I barely scraped together a career after she was born."

Lola's shoulders shook as she fell into the first sob. Susan wrapped her arm around her shoulders and squeezed her against her.

"I just don't know how this happened," Lola whispered.

"Accidents happen," Susan said. "And this is one of the happiest kind of accidents! Imagine if you hadn't had Audrey all these years. Your life would be so much emptier than it is now. She's the thing you love the most in this world, right? And now, she's going to have her own baby. It doesn't have to be a bad thing, Lola."

Lola squeezed her eyes shut. "I just wanted so much more for her. I wanted her to do everything on her own terms, in her own time. This isn't the '90s anymore. You have to make huge strides in your career very early. Audrey and I had a plan and a solid one. She was going to work in New York. She looks just like Mom; she has a face for television. Heck, she could be anything she wants. And now—" Lola's hands came up and cupped her head as she started to cry again.

Susan and Lola huddled together. Susan drummed up a few more comments, none of which seemed to soothe Lola's immense sadness. Most of them had the ring of, "Having children is one of the most beautiful things you can do in your life. You know that, Lola. And now, Audrey will know that, too."

Suddenly, Christine bolted up from the picnic table. She was filled with panic, sadness, and fear and it swirled in her stomach, making her suddenly nauseous. She knew this wasn't her battle to wage; this wasn't her moment of personal sadness. However, all this talk of the "goodness" and "giving birth, and creating life," nearly destroyed her. She knew that would never be in her future. Neither Susan nor Lola paid her any attention as she headed inside, unstable on her feet. From the door, she hollered out, "I'm going to take a drive. Call me if you need anything." Neither of her sisters answered.

They were mothers, beyond anything else. Jake, Amanda, Audrey: those were the people who mattered the most to them. Christine hovered somewhere below. She couldn't blame them for that.

She just couldn't relate to it.

CHAPTER 9

CHRISTINE GRABBED THE KEYS TO ONE OF THE INN CARS AND leaped into the front seat. When she revved the engine, an old Bob Seger song blared through the speakers, the sounds of long ago summers on Martha's Vineyard. As she eased through the greying forests and the winding roads, she had only the slightest comprehension of where she wanted to go. The first few buildings at the edge of Edgartown surprised her. She gripped the steering wheel hard, her knuckles turning white. As she parked the car on a side road, she whispered, "Get ahold of yourself. You're just going to a normal bar for a drink. It's not a big deal."

When she stepped out of the car, she swept her fingers through her hair and drew her shoulders back. Down at the end of the alley, in a little park, several Edgartown tourists collected in a circle around what looked like a marriage proposal. She watched as a handsome, early 30s suited-up man perched down on one knee, while his future blonde bride beamed out a 'yes' after he proposed. Christine, who had witnessed more proposals in her early days on Martha's Vineyard than she could count, rolled her eyes and turned the other way. There was optimism, happiness, hope, but she was headed elsewhere— to the darkened, shadowy bar, where her dead mother's ex-lover drank himself to death.

The oldest Edgartown Bar had now been upgraded inside to appeal to the locals and tourists, although it still kept many of its old design. Located next to some new buildings that were shinier, the rough exterior still scared off some of the faint at heart. Although, outside kept its rustic appeal, and in some areas on the inside kept its original appeal that hinted at the long history of spirited delights.

The bar was to the left of the door with wrap around seating, featuring jars of 75-cent pickled eggs that sat on the counter, and a few square tables, four chairs each, to the right. There were a couple of high-top tables along a line of windows facing the water, and another larger dining room with more tables and booths at the back. Brick walls, wooden beams, and white shiplap walls and ceilings adorned the space, plus plenty of televisions for anyone who was there for the broadcast entertainment.

There were more vibrant colors at the front of the bar, but once you made your way back to the booths and tables, it became dark and dingy, giving you a nostalgic feeling of the relic it had once been back in the day.

A woman in her late fifties or sixties entered the bar area. She had been seated with another lady, playing Scrabble, killing time. She placed her elbows on the bar and said, "What can I do for you, beautiful?"

Christine gave a slight smile. The woman seemed genuine if a little raggedy. "I'll have a vodka tonic," she said. "Please."

"Coming right up."

Christine waited at the edge of the bar while the woman made her drink. As her eyes adjusted to the bleary light, she scanned the room. Two older guys, both wearing baseball hats, sat at one of the corner booths, stewing over their beers. A woman around Christine's age sat with a glass of wine at a tall table by one of the windows, which looked like it had been sealed from the outside with logs. On the walls were what seemed like hundreds of framed photographs from decades earlier.

The sound of the glass on the bar counter made Christine jumped. She turned to look at the bartender who smiled to show she had lost a tooth on the right side. "That'll be five dollars, honey."

After Christine paid, she walked toward the photographs on the main wall, many of which were in black frames. As she scanned over the long-forgotten faces, the husbands and wives in celebration, their glasses lifted toward whoever took the photograph, she felt hazy with nostalgia and sadness. The Edgartown Bar now seemed upgraded to what the owners could afford. If she wasn't mistaken, she caught sight of the bartender, maybe twenty years before, in one of the photographs: much thinner and prettier, her hands on her hips, wearing an old apron that said, "Don't Mess With The Bartender."

Stan Ellis, as she had once known him, aged mid-thirties, was featured in two of the photos. In one, he had his arm strung around another guy's shoulders, while the other guy held up a massive fish, recently caught. They both grinned madly, and their cheeks were sunburnt from the long day of fishing. This was the man her mother had loved. This was the version of him, anyway.

To Christine's disappointment, her mother wasn't featured in any of the photographs. She supposed her mom had been too careful for something like that to give her affair away.

Someone else entered the bar. Footsteps crept from the door to the bar counter, while Christine remained poised near the photographs. Every part of Christine's body felt taut, panicked; after all, she suspected Stan would enter at any moment, but she didn't have any kind of plan for what she would do when she saw him. Accost him? Demand to know why he had ruined her life?

But could she fully blame Stan Ellis for her ruined life at this point?

"Christine Sheridan? Is that you?"

The voice rang out near the bar and chilled her to the bone. Slowly, she turned to the familiar sound, her nostrils flared. There, holding a large beer and standing in a near-perfect white v-neck shirt and a pair of jeans that made him look like a Calvin Klein model, stood Zach Walters. His blue eyes caught whatever light lurked in that dank place, and his smile snuck up toward his ears. He was both glad to see her and clearly confused.

"Are you stalking me?" Christine asked, arching a perfectly manicured eyebrow. A hint of a smile played at the corners of her mouth; however, she refused to let it show.

"Excuse me, but I think it should be the other way around," Zach said. "I live in Edgartown. This is my bar."

Christine glanced toward the bartender, who gave a half-shrug and added, "He does. We put up with him."

"I imagine it must be a difficult thing to do," Christine smirked.

"Rita, meet my high school nemesis, Christine Sheridan," Zach said.

"I know who she is," Rita said.

Christine arched her brow.

"Come on. Everyone knows who the Sheridan girls are," Rita said, sounding annoyed. "You don't think I'm stupid, do you?" She turned swiftly toward the back room, muttering to herself.

At this, Christine had to laugh. She glanced at Zach again, who chuckled and said, "This is Rita's place. We have to play by Rita's rules."

Christine couldn't take her eyes off Zach. They sat across from one another at one of the back booths, and she cupped her vodka tonic with both hands, feeling like a teenager. Was it possible that he was more handsome than the last time she had seen him? He tilted his head a bit, rubbing the back of his neck, and said, "Good lord, today was a tough one. We had this enormous dinner rush. Chelsea Clinton was there with a few of her college friends, and the security was over the top."

"What did Chelsea Clinton order?" Christine asked.

"Salmon lasagna," Zach said. "It's a new specialty we added at the bistro, although we've been experimenting a lot with new menu items."

Christine shrugged. "I think what we've always featured at the bistro has worked well."

"But you know what it's like. It's my first full year there soon, and I want to feel like I've made it my own," Zach returned.

"But it's not really yours, is it? I mean, it's my father's. It's the Sunrise Cove Inn's bistro. Better to go for the profits than an experiment for your own vanity," Christine said.

Zach's blue eyes grew icy. He drank his beer and returned the glass with a clank on the table. "Always a pleasure to run into you, Christine."

"I mean, sure. I know what it's like to open your own place," Christine continued. She felt her anger flare-up, the old familiar kind she had always had toward Zach.

"I mean, you don't, right? That wasn't your place..."

"But Chez Frank was so much of mine," Christine insisted. "I helped switch the menu around all the time. As a head pastry chef, I had to coordinate everything so that the desserts matched with the mains. It was hectic work, but it was collaborative and it was..."

Zach chuckled. Christine felt all the blood rush to her cheeks.

"Why are you laughing?" she demanded.

"You just don't know anything about how I operate at the bistro, and you want to pick it apart. It's just like you always did in high school," Zach stated as he leaned back against the booth cushion. "You were always such a judgmental creature. You never let anyone pin you down."

Christine reached up and rubbed her eyes. Exhaustion engulfed her like a blanket. "I'm sorry. I am. You're right. I don't know anything about what you're doing over there. Funny, also, I was just reading my mom's diary from when I was around thirteen or fourteen and she said a lot of what you just did. I was always such an angsty wreck."

Zach lifted his empty beer mug. "Hear, hear," he said. "To being an angst wreck."

Christine chuckled as she clinked her glass with his. "What the hell would you know about it? You seem like you've got it all together. Your own kind of bistro and your music. You probably have a beautiful house here in Edgartown, and so many friends, and...." She trailed off as his eyes grew hazy.

"Well, Christine. In the interest of honesty, no. I haven't had it altogether so easy," Zach said. His voice was light, but Christine could sense some mystery weaved within his words.

"What do you mean?" She tilted her head, curious.

Zach gave a light shrug. "Let's just say it's been a meandering road before now— a twisting, dark road with a lot of potholes."

"I'm sorry to hear that," Christine said. Her heart thumped a little bit faster. "I can relate. But you know that already, I guess." She swallowed a lump in her throat and added, "I would tell you, you can talk to me about whatever happened, but I imagine that I'm not first on your list of people to talk to about anything like that; or anything at all, really."

"And yet, here we are together," he stated.

"Indeed. We're so lucky," Christine said, smiling through the sarcasm.

The door to the bar opened again. Slowly, Christine lifted her gaze in that direction. There, standing in the doorway, was Stan Ellis. He was stooped forward a bit, his wild hair showing bits of scalp beneath, his dark eyes brooding and his beard thick. Those eyes found Christine's immediately as he stood there, like some sort of horrendous, terrifying, fisherman statue.

Christine knew that he recognized her. She matched his gaze for a long time. Zach balked, didn't say anything, and turned to see Stan. It seemed as though all the air in the bar had been sucked out.

Suddenly, Stan yanked himself around, grabbed the handle of the door, and rushed back outside. Christine bolted after him.

"Christine! What are you doing?" Zach called after her.

But Christine wouldn't have stopped for anyone, least of all Zach Walters. She charged for the door, ripped it open, and rushed toward the back alley. Just when she reached it, Stan revved the engine of his truck. The wheels raced across the alley bricks and shot him out onto the street. He moved so quickly; several tourists cried out, "Watch out!" Christine staggered toward the street and watched as he drove out of Edgartown, away from her and his ghost of the past.

Christine felt like a shell of a person when she returned to the bar. Zach hustled up to her, smearing his fingers through his hair. "What was that about?" he demanded.

Christine ignored him and walked to the bar. She lifted two fingers to Rita and said, "Can I have two shots of tequila? Please."

Rita nodded and poured. The stereo played Bruce Springsteen's "Born in the USA" while she drank the two shots back immediately, one after another, with Zach watching her in bewilderment. Finally, after she finished the last, Zach lifted two fingers to Rita and ordered the same.

"If you're going on this journey, I don't want you to go alone," he said. Yet again, he delivered the most handsome smile Christine had ever seen.

If she had been a different version of herself, she might have kissed him right then. A wilder, more provocative, more interesting version rather than the washed-up and confused Christine she was now.

By the end of that half-hour, Christine and Zach hovered over the counter, begging and pleading Rita to change the music to their favorite tracks. They had both had four shots of tequila, and the night seemed glossy and filled with promise. Unfortunately for them, it was already quite late, and Rita confessed she couldn't keep the bar open only for them.

"Not even for Christine? One of the famous Sheridan sisters?" Zach asked.

"Not even for the Queen of England," Rita affirmed.

"You know, Rita, me and Zach actually hate each other," Christine said, her voice bubbling with laughter.

"Do you? I really couldn't care less," Rita smirked with her hands on each of her hips.

Christine hiccuped and tossed her head back. "Susan and Lola would hate that I'm doing this. Hate it."

"Why?" Zach asked as he scrunched his brows together.

"I don't know. I think they would think I was going off the rails again."

"Well, aren't you?" Zach shrugged and tilted his head.

"I don't know. Maybe. Maybe it's what I need to do right now, so soon after everything fell apart," Christine said. "Susan's life fell apart, and she immediately went to work, putting our family back together again. But me? My life falls apart, and all I want to do is drink at a dingy bar at the edge of Edgartown. No offense, Rita."

"None taken," Rita said.

Christine sighed and dropped her head onto her fist, her elbow on the bar. "Lola is going to be a grandmother. She's only thirty-eight years old."

"Wow. You Sheridan women really get to work, don't you?" Zach said.

"My sisters do, anyway. Not me, though. But maybe it's better that way. None of my depressive DNA gets passed on to the next generation," Christine murmured. "Maybe I got it from my mother. And maybe it ends with me."

"That's just silly talk, Christine," Zach stated.

"I feel like I am as old as the Nantucket Sound," Christine said playfully. "As ancient as the sandy beach."

"Now you're just being dramatic," Zach said.

"Maybe." She pondered for a moment, recognizing how lost her thoughts had gotten, yet allowing them to flow.

Finally, Rita convinced them to leave the bar. Zach called Christine a taxi, saying he would hand-deliver her car the following day. They waited outside together as the moon fluttered in and out of focus, behind the clouds. When the taxi arrived, Zach placed his hand on her lower back to help her inside.

"You know I don't need your help, Zach," Christine said as she adjusted her seatbelt over her waist.

"I know. I'm just trying to pretend to be a good guy," Zach returned.

"Well, don't. I can see right through it," Christine said. She wasn't entirely sure if she was joking or not, but Zach laughed anyway.

"See you tomorrow, Christine. And the next day—and the next."

"What a life to look forward to," she said, rolling her eyes. "Good night."

CHAPTER 10

For the big fifteenth birthday celebration, Christine decided to prepare a multi-layered French cake with magazine-ready frosting decorations and lavender lemon icing. It was a variation on a recipe she had made frequently at Chez Frank, one that had made Chrissy Teigen's jaw drop with pleasure when she had come in for a visit. It had been featured on countless food and dining magazine covers and for a very brief amount of time, it had been called "Christine's Creation in the Upper West Side." When Christine had first created this cake, she had been in the prime of her life, happier than ever.

Now, of course, she was a bit like a lost ship at sea.

Regardless, she wanted to share this delicacy with her family and, admittedly, show off a bit. So, the day before the party, she found herself at the Sunrise Cove Inn itself, in a little lace apron, hovering over the counter at the bistro. It was an hour after the lunch rush, and Zach Walters was in a surprisingly good mood, making jokes with the busboys and servers and asking Christine if she needed anything.

"Just a little more space, Zach," Christine said, laughing as he hovered a bit too close to her.

"We did fantastic today, Christine," Zach said, seemingly not hearing her. "I came up with this new recipe for gazpacho and one of the guests actually ran in here asking if she could have the directions... she lost her mind when I said *no*." He chuckled to himself, then rushed to the side of the kitchen, grabbed himself one of the IPAs they kept in the little back fridge, and popped the top. Christine kept her eye on him and, moments later, he performed the same action for her.

"I know better than to drink in front of Christine Sheridan without getting her one," he said, clinking his bottle with hers.

"Brooklyn Brewing Company," Christine said, analyzing the bottle. "I used to date a brewer there. That was a crazy time of my life."

"Did he have a full beard, and was he burly with tattoo's like all the other brewers in the world?" Zach asked jokingly.

"I guess. They're all like that, aren't they?" Christine giggled as she poured flour into a mixing bowl.

Zach eventually left the kitchen that afternoon, as he had the evening off. Christine fell into a kind of daydream as she baked the cake: sipping her IPA, chatting with the waiters and busboys, occasionally checking on the food they had made and surprising herself with how much she respected the menu.

"I've worked here about two years," one of the busboys, named Ronnie, told her. "And Zach is seriously the best. I've tried almost everything on the menu, and I would die for all of it."

Ronnie was a red-headed seventeen-year-old with, it seemed, a lot of laughter, a lot of banter, and a lot of eagerness also, to taste the batter of her French cake. She clucked her tongue each time and said, "No, no. I'm not that kind of baker. I'm a professional. Go taste your mom's cookie dough, and leave mine out of it."

Ronnie laughed. "You're just like Zach. So serious about the craft, or whatever."

When the layers baked, Christine decided to taste-test some of the pastries and baked breads the bistro had on-hand, both for sale and awaiting tomorrow's early-morning sale to various tourists, which they did through a little side window out of the kitchen. She was surprised to note how much they lacked in flavor, that the texture was almost soggy when it should have been flaky. For such a gorgeous bistro, with beautiful colors on the walls and stunning seaside light and inventive recipes, it seemed a shame that it had such lackluster pastries.

But did she dare say this to Zach?

After the layers were finished, she stored them and returned back home for the evening. When she arrived, she found Lola in yet another frantic conversation with Audrey. She sat in the porch swing, her long hair up in a ponytail that was a tad haphazard, as she clutched her phone to her ear. Christine grabbed a glass of wine and sat with Susan and their father in the living room.

"How is she doing?" Christine asked.

"Audrey and Lola seem like the same person," Susan said with a heavy sigh. "Both of them are very, very intelligent and very, very stubborn women."

"Sounds like all the Sheridan girls," Wes said with a chuckle.

"What's going to happen?" Christine asked, arching a brow.

"Audrey is going to come here, I think. Next week," Susan explained. "She's going to finish out her internship and then fly out. This house is going to be crammed full."

"The more, the merrier!" Wes said.

"Scott's already talking about building onto the place," Susan said. "As if he didn't have enough on his plate. He's really taken to work at the Inn, though. I swear that man has more patience than God himself. Today, dealing with some particularly annoying customers, he calmed everyone down so much that he eventually went to lunch with them. They swapped numbers and might become friends! I've never seen anything like it."

"Dad, you were always like that," Christine said. "With people at the Inn."

"It was my life," Wes affirmed. "But to be honest with you, now that I have more time to myself, I don't miss it as much as I thought I would."

"Scott and Dad and I went for a walk through the woods this afternoon," Susan said. "Dad, you showed us that particular kind of bird. What was it again?"

"Oh, right. A Killdeer bird," Wes said.

The following afternoon, Susan manned the front desk at the Inn as Christine entered to tend to the cake. Christine wore a pair of black flats, a jean miniskirt, and a tank-top that highlighted her long arms and shoulders. Susan seemed to study Christine for a moment before saying, "You look dressed up today."

"Just for the party later," Christine said. "I know it's not a Manhattan high-rise apartment, but it is family. I want to look nice."

"I see," Susan said with a smile.

"By the way, I wanted to say it's incredible that Dad remembers that kind of bird, and not, like, where he put the keys or what year it is," Christine said. "I don't know how the mind is ordered, but it's a strange thing, isn't it?"

Susan nodded. "He can whip out memories of us when we were little girls like it's nobody's business, but yesterday, he called me Kerry again. I don't know what to do with him. The doctor said his mind is going to steadily float away from us like this."

"Strange," Christine said.

Scott entered the lobby area, coming out of the office where their mother and father had once operated on connected desks, manning the everyday happenings of the Sunrise Cove Inn. Now, the torch had been passed.

"Hey, Christine! How you been?" Scott asked. He stepped behind the front desk and stamped a kiss on Susan's cheek, making her blush.

They really couldn't keep their hands off one another. It was like they were teenagers all over again.

"Just have to go finish up the girls' cake," Christine said. "Not every day you turn fifteen, you know?"

Back in the kitchen, Zach was nowhere to be found. The lunch rush had already stormed itself across the kitchen, and the busboy, Ronnie, panted in the corner, giving Christine a bright smile.

"Zach just took a walk, but he'll be back soon," he said. "We had some YouTube star in here this afternoon. I served her. She reviews hotels and stuff like that."

"Wow," Christine said, pretending to be impressed. "That's crazy."

She mixed up the lavender-lemon frosting lovingly, enjoying

how it felt to do this same action again and again: the perfect twirling of her wrist, the feeling of the ingredients coming together. She had always felt it was something like the maestro in front of the orchestra forcing all the separate "instruments" together to create a beautiful end result.

Ronnie watched as she piled the cake layers high, smearing frosting on each layer as she topped it off. The cake was to be nearly two feet tall, the kind of thing her Aunt Kerry and Uncle Trevor would obviously brag about, and the kind of thing the girls would always remember. It wasn't like Christine could give them second cousins to play with, but she would give them some damn good cake that they would both remember for the rest of their lives.

Slowly, delicately, she began to form little flowers across the cake: keeping such focus, that she stuck her tongue out and bit down on it. Ronnie came in and out of the kitchen, complaining that the rush continued. At six, they planned to shut down the terrace-area to hold the girls' birthday party. Still, they would keep some seats in the bistro open for stragglers.

Christine added the finishing touches to the cake and took a step back. It was absolutely glorious. Far better than anything she had crafted in Manhattan, something she almost wanted to snap a pic of to share with some of her online foody buddies. As she beamed at it, Zach entered the kitchen, whistling, wearing another pair of perfect jeans, his chest puffed out and his dark blonde hair swept back.

"My God," he said when he spotted the cake. "Don't tell me you are the secret behind this, Christine Sheridan."

Christine laughed. "I am. I'm sorry."

"It's absolutely extraordinary," Zach beamed. His face fell as he wandered around it, analyzing it from all sides. "I've really never seen anything like this outside of Paris. Seriously—you could bake with the greats."

"That's nothing on how it tastes," Christine said. "It's positively... orgasmic."

"What a word choice," Zach said, his eyes flashing.

Christine blushed profusely. She felt as though the ground beneath her was uneasy. Slowly, Zach reached for the base of the cake tray and lifted it. "I just want to see the detail," he said. He stepped a bit to the side, tilting the cake, analyzing the little roses, the pivots within each petal. Christine was overwhelmed with pleasure at her work being regarded in this way.

But suddenly, the swinging-door that burst out from the dining room and into the kitchen came open. Ronnie, exhausted and strung-out from his long day at the bistro, entered and immediately rammed into Zach. Zach's lips burst open in surprise. The cake fell forward, as did Zach, as did Ronnie, smacking layer after layer across both Zach and Christine.

Christine closed her eyes and fell to her knees. Devastation was the word for it— devastation and anger, and defeat. For the past twenty-four hours, all she'd done was put her heart and soul into this cake. And now, here it was: smeared across her and Zach and even partially on Ronnie.

With her hands clenched, Christine stood there on her knees, her eyes closed and her tongue slowly licked the frosting on her lip. What was she going to do? The party was in three hours and the one thing she had wanted to provide was lying all over her and the floor.

CHAPTER 11

"Zach?" Christine said his name toward the ground, blinking so that bits of icing frosted her eyelashes. "Zach, I cannot stress this enough. What. Did. You. Do?" She let out a low sigh.

Ronnie spewed, crying, "Oh my, God! I'm so, so sorry, Christine. I had no idea he was standing there, and I just... we have such a crowded floor right now and I..."

The kid's fear was palpable. Slowly, she lifted her head to peer up at both Zach and Ronnie, side-by-side. Both of them glowed with white light, due to the icing on her eyelashes. It looked like she was about to enter heaven. Ronnie's face was absolutely petrified, but Zach's? Zach's made it seem like this was the greatest day of his life.

She should have known that somehow, someway, he would find a way to ruin her. She just hadn't assumed it would feel so personal when it happened. She pressed one of her hands to the ground and then lifted herself up by the counter.

"Do you need help?" Ronnie said. He sprung forward, grabbing her elbow clumsily, which only ended up making it more difficult to stand.

"Thanks, Ronnie," she said. She splayed her hand across the counter and looked at the dead carcass of the cake between herself and Zach. It had landed across her face and upper body before smashing down head-first. Lavender and lemon frosting was smeared everywhere.

Silence stretched between them. Christine swallowed the lump in her throat, shoving it down, and turned her gaze to Zach. She probably looked like some kind of maniac covered in frosting.

"What on earth gave you the impression that you could just lift my multi-tiered creation into the air like that?" she said in bitter haste. She was at her wits' end.

Almost immediately, Ronnie had sensed that the blame hadn't been cast on him, so he took a moment to shoot back out onto the busy floor leaving the two to battle it out.

"You speak like you just painted the Mona Lisa," Zach said.

"It took me an entire day to make that cake," Christine spewed. "It was once called the best piece of cake in Manhattan, and I wanted to share it with my family after so many, many years away from them."

"Now, you're going to point the guilt of you staying away for so long at me, too?" Zach returned. His blue eyes were dangerously dark.

"I mean, part of the reason I did stay away from this island for so long was because of people like you," Christine spat. "Self-righteous Vineyard people who think the entire world revolves around them."

"You'll really never get over that, will you?" Zach said with an obnoxious laugh.

Christine sputtered. They hadn't talked about what had happened all those years ago yet, not really, and this was his second or third mention that he remembered it in any kind of detail. She smashed her arms over her chest and crossed them in frustration.

She should just go back to the house, shower off, and head back to New York.

She could crash at a friend's place in Brooklyn until she figured out what to do next.

Audrey and Lola, Amanda and Susan, Scott and Zach and everyone else could go on living their lives. All of them happy— so sure of themselves and their future.

All she'd wanted to do was make the perfect cake for her niece's.

"You're impossible," she whispered, her voice catching in her throat.

Before she knew what he'd done, Zach drew a line down her cheek, through the icing, and then dotted the lavender lemon icing across his tongue. Christine's lips parted in shock. Suddenly, however, the darkness behind Zach's eyes cleared. He arched his brow and said, "Is that lavender lemon?"

Christine's heart thumped. She could feel her anger rising with each second that ticked past. "Yes. Of course, it is. What else would it be?"

"No, no. I know. It's just so unique. I've had these flavors together before, but this... it really does taste every bit as good as something I've had in Paris or Rome or Stockholm."

"Now you're just bragging about all the places you've been," Christine said.

"Maybe a bit. But really, Christine. This is extraordinary."

Christine was a bit shocked at how genuine he sounded. She grabbed a paper towel from the counter and wiped it across her face, forehead, and bits of her hair, then dropped her hands to her side.

"Listen," Zach tried. "Why don't we bake something up really quickly? Something a bit smaller, a bit less complicated, but no less delicious."

To her intense humiliation, a tiny tear dropped out of the side of her eye and skated through the leftover icing.

"Seriously," Zach said. "I'll help you every step of the way."

Somehow rejuvenated, Christine stepped into the little bathroom connected to the kitchen. She looked at herself in the mirror and scrubbed off the remaining bits of icing from her face, clothes, and hair. She then added the tiniest bit of lipstick and eyeliner, blinked at herself, and told her racing heart to calm down. That is was an accident and everything would work out just fine. However, she felt like she was still going to have a breakdown right there on the spot.

By the time she returned to the kitchen, the cake had been removed and the floor scrubbed. Zach stood, cleaned up, with a fresh apron, and passed another one to Christine. Ingredients were placed out on the gleaming countertop, and a radio in the corner played a soft rock song.

"You've really set the mood, haven't you?" Christine said, surprising herself with her ability to laugh.

"Baking is a delicate thing," he said with a wink. "You can't make a cake while angry. It'll turn out stale."

"That sounds like witchcraft to me," Christine said, drawing her hair into a messy bun and diving toward the flour.

Very quickly, they prepared a simple vanilla cake. As it baked, Christine stirred up another batch of lavender and lemon icing and made little flowers to be put on top of the cake. Although it would only have two layers, it was certainly big enough for the twenty guests who would be in attendance. The fancy French icing would assuredly make a good impression, as well.

About a half-hour before six, Aunt Kerry and Uncle Trevor arrived to start the decorating process out on the terrace overlooking the water. Christine finished the last detail on the top of the cake and walked out to greet them and help them blow up and tie balloons to picnic tables. Throughout, Aunt Kerry and Uncle Trevor bickered slightly about where to put which decorations, how to assemble the tables and chairs. It was oddly adorable, if only because this bickering represented how much they cared for their granddaughters.

The guests began to arrive a little after six. Abby and Gail wore matching blue sailor dresses and wore their hair long. They stood near the entrance to the terrace and greeted everyone with a hug, accepting presents and cards and then helped place them on a little table. As guests arrived, they ordered drinks from the bistro bartender off to the right, who had been hired for this exclusive party for the night.

Christine watched from near the bartender stand as Abby and Gail brought their arms around their dearest friends, jumped up and down in excitement and took some selfies with one another.

It was crazy. Fifteen years old. When she had turned fifteen, her mother had already been dead. She hadn't felt reason enough to take many photos during those last few summers she had spent on the island, especially as it had seemed as though she'd always run quickly through her friends, getting into silly fights and losing them for good. "Christine is just a bit harder around edges than most," she'd heard her dad say once to a friend. "We don't know what to do with her. I'm sure she will come around."

On this thought, Wes, Lola, Susan, and Scott entered the party. Susan, naturally, held the present and passed it to Abby. The family had gotten them tons of beauty supplies, which Lola had had a field day picking them out. "When you're fifteen, you're ready to show the world what you're made of!" she'd said.

Susan approached with a vibrant smile. "There you are! I thought I'd see you earlier. How did it go with the cake?"

Christine heaved a sigh and told the story as quickly as she could. Susan scrunched her nose. "But you managed to make something else?"

"Yes. Zach helped," Christine explained.

"You must be disappointed," Susan said. "But the girls are fifteen. They're used to eating stuff like pop tarts."

"I know. I just wanted to..." She shrugged as Lola approached, walking quickly, her gorgeous hair windswept.

"Hey!" she said. She dotted a kiss on Christine's cheek and said, "My dear, I'm in such a fluster. I got Audrey's ticket booked this morning and made her a doctor's appointment for next week. I don't know anything about the doctors on the island, but I guess this is better than nothing?"

"They seem to take good care of Dad," Susan offered.

"Right." Lola's eyes seemed far away.

"You must be excited to see her," Christine tried.

Lola's eyes cut toward her. She gave her a terrible look, one that seemed to translate just how little Christine could possibly understand the situation, given the fact that she wasn't a mother.

"I want to wring her neck, but yes, I've missed her," she said simply. She then turned back to Susan and began a separate conversation about new developments in pregnancy and childbirth. Susan furrowed her brow and answered in kind. Again, they built a wall between themselves and Christine.

But there was so much to be grateful for at the party. Christine grabbed another glass of wine and sat with her father, Aunt Kerry, and Uncle Trevor, as everyone dug into the chicken tacos, which Zach had prepared for the occasion. The conversation was light and cheerful. Even Wes engaged with her a tiny bit more, something that Christine had always felt was more reserved for Susan or Lola.

After dinner, Uncle Trevor carried the cake outside and splayed it between the twin girls, who stood on either side of a picnic table. Their eyes glowed as he lit the candles. All the guests, from their family to their dearest school friends, sang 'Happy Birthday,' and then, the girls reached across the table, gripped one another's hands, closed their eyes, and blew on the candles at the same time. It was like they had to be united in all things, even in their wishes. Immediately after, everyone erupted into cheers, and the cake was sliced.

Wes pointed at his slice with his fork, his mouth filled with lavender lemon icing. "You made this, Christine?" he asked.

"I did," Christine said.

"It's a miracle," he said. "I think they'll have to wheel me out of here, but I'm getting another slice."

Christine stood to grab another glass of wine. On her way to the bartender, she spotted Zach, leaning against the side of the Inn with a beer in his hand. He cut her one of those ridiculously handsome smiles again and said, "You did good today, kid."

"Ha. No thanks to you," she replied. After a strange pause, she added, "Actually, no. I don't mean that. Thank you for helping me put together the cake. I don't know what I would have done without you—maybe a grocery store cake or something. All I know is I would have been ruined as a pastry chef for good."

Zach chuckled. "Don't mention it. But it did get me thinking about something."

"What's that?"

"If I know you at all, I know you probably tasted our pastries and baked bread while you've been here," he said.

"I plead the fifth," Christine said, putting both her hands up as if he pointed a gun at her.

"That's what I thought. And I know you know how— shall we say, lacking they are? But I don't want it to be like that anymore now that you're back on the island," he continued. "I have a vision for this place. I want us to be the go-to bakery on the island. But I need a top-level pastry chef to join the bistro. Someone extremely talented, someone like you."

Christine's eyebrows rocketed up her forehead. She had not seen this coming.

"Obviously, you can think about it," Zach said. "But since we're already mid-way through July, sooner, rather than later, would be better for everyone. The hours are long, but the people who work here are spectacular."

"Oh? The people who own the Inn?" Christine said with a smile. "I think I might have heard of them."

"That's the kind of sass and sarcasm I need behind my pastry chef," Zach affirmed. "Say you'll work for me. Pretty please."

CHAPTER 12

Hours before the crack of dawn Monday morning, Christine marched into the gleaming kitchen at the Sunrise Cove Inn bistro and snapped on the lights. It was her mission to have freshly baked croissants, baguettes, and French pastries like tartes aux pommes sold to the morning crowd, which she thought would be enough to generate a buzz across Oak Bluffs. She had done this sort of thing before and now, the idea of pouring that love back into the Sunrise Cove Inn thrilled her and gave her a new spark. She felt as though her mother, despite all her confusion about her teenage angst and darker years, would have been proud.

By eight in the morning, after several hours of tireless, soul-affirming work, Christine displayed her glorious results in the little glass display case near the cash register, along with some in the little case near the back walk-up window connected to the kitchen. As she placed the final, fluffy-buttery croissant in the window, she heard Zach call, "My god. I feel like I've walked into heaven. The smells in here are amazing."

Immediately, Christine's lips purred into a smile. She turned to find the handsome man saunter through the kitchen, preheating the oven and beaming.

"They look fantastic," he told her. "Thank you for starting right away."

"I had to save this place. It was drowning without me," she said with a laugh.

Christine walked Zach toward the back counter, where she had outlined the dessert offerings for the day. "I have three pecan pies baking right now, and I noticed you have buckets of vanilla ice cream in the walk-in freezer. Another option—" She yanked the oven open to reveal gooey chocolate brownies.

"Wow. You really went all out," he said, impressed. "How do you keep track of everything?"

"My little secret, I guess," Christine said brightly.

That morning, just before the breakfast rush, Christine signed a tentative contract with Sunrise Cove Inn bistro and then headed to the lobby to find Natalie behind the counter.

"Susan had me come in at the last minute," she said. "I guess your niece is about to arrive, so it's a little chaotic at home."

"Shoot," Christine said. "I completely forgot about that."

In a hurry, Christine stepped out of the Inn and walked the forest path toward the house. The moment she arrived, one of the Inn vehicles charged up the driveway, clicking across the gravel. Audrey sat in the front seat, a perfect, spitting image of teenage Lola. When she drew open the car door, her eyes connected with Christine's. Her smile was strained. It looked as though she had cried all the way from Chicago to the steps of their family home.

"Hey, Audrey," Christine said. She gave her what she hoped was a tender, understanding smile. What she wanted to say was: *I know what it's like when nothing goes your way. I know what it's like when the world turns on its axis and you feel like you're left behind.* But she hardly knew her niece at all and didn't want to give any unsolicited advice. She would have hated that at nineteen.

Back in the house, Susan laid out several croissants, which she had apparently picked up from the Inn while Christine had been busy finalizing the pecan pies.

"Here she is! Our beautiful girl," Susan said, collecting Audrey in a hug.

Lola collapsed on the couch and scrubbed her fingers through her hair. She looked as though she hadn't slept a wink all night.

"Thanks, Aunt Susie," Audrey said. "Those look amazing."

"They taste amazing. Christine made them before anyone on the planet woke up this morning. Have one," Susan told her. "The pot of coffee is almost ready. You stayed at a hotel in Falmouth last night, didn't you?" She shuffled toward the coffee pot as she spoke, reminding Christine that she was a woman who would multitask to get anything done.

"Yeah. It was weird to stay there alone," Audrey said.

"Who is that?" Wes called from the bottom of the staircase as he crept into the room.

"Are you just waking up, Dad?" Christine asked, shocked, as Wes had always been one to wake up around five.

"Felt a little tired this morning," Wes said, shrugging it off. "Wanted to rest up to see my grandbaby. Audrey, welcome!"

Susan's eyes flashed toward Christine's. Together, they seemed to have the same thought: yet again, their dad had surprised them with his memory. Maybe the puzzles were working.

"Good to see you again, Grandpa," Audrey said. She stood and gave Wes a half-hug, then fell back in the chair again and collected a tiny piece of croissant off the flaky top and placed it on her tongue. Her shoulders fell forward. "Do you guys mind if I take a walk by the water?"

It was clear that she wasn't ready to talk just yet, although that was all Lola wanted out of her. The Sheridan sisters exchanged glances, until Lola said, "Of course, honey. Take all the time you need."

Susan poured Audrey's cup of coffee into a portable canister mug. The sisters and Wes watched as she snuck out the porch door and then walked slowly down the stairs and the hill that led to the water. To Christine, Audrey seemed like a shell of who she had been only a few weeks before. Whatever had happened in Chicago, it had hollowed her out.

"Did she say anything to you on the drive?" Susan asked Lola.

"She said she wasn't ready to talk yet," Lola said. "Which I understand. She just finished the internship and only just got back to the east coast. But I'm dying to understand. What went wrong? Why did she do this? I just..." She pressed her palm to her forehead and shook her head slowly. "It makes my head spin."

Although Christine had been up for hours, she simmered with a ridiculous amount of energy. Instead of heading up for a nap, like she'd planned, she scrubbed up the kitchen and washed the sheets on all the beds. Lola, in a kind of catatonic state on the living room sofa, hardly noticed. Wes perched at the breakfast table in front of another puzzle, and, as Christine marched past with a vacuum in hand, she clicked a few pieces into place.

"He needs to do it himself," Lola said into her hands, just loud enough for both of them to hear.

Wes's face crumpled. Immediately, Lola pressed her hands into her eyes and whispered, "I'm sorry. I'm sorry. Whatever. It doesn't matter. I'm going upstairs."

Around lunchtime, Christine stepped behind the stove and prepared a big vat of white cheddar macaroni and cheese. It had been the girls' favorites when they'd been younger, something Christine had messed around with, varying up the spices and creaminess levels since she had gone to culinary school. The first smells of it brought Susan back in from the front porch.

"Don't tell me you're making mac and cheese," Susan said. Her groan was fake, just something left over from her old Newark life.

"I guess you haven't had it in years, right?" Christine asked.

"Nope." Susan pressed her hand against her lower stomach, still flat, and said, "This place has really destroyed my long-standing avoidance of carbs."

"Better get used to it, baby," Christine said with a laugh.

"You're in a good mood," Susan said, arching her brow.

Christine shrugged. Throughout her life, she'd hated it when people pointed out her mood, as though whatever she had done needed to be approved by the grand committee. Still, she was in a good mood, probably as a result of her newfound position at the Inn. She had a purpose again.

Out on the back porch, the Sheridan sisters, Audrey, and Wes gathered around bowls of macaroni and cheese. Although it was late July, the sky was strangely overcast, the grey clouds thick. Christine reached for a bottle of cabernet and poured herself a tall glass, something that brought frowns from both Susan and Lola. Since when was she not allowed to drink with lunch? She had worked all day, hadn't she?

After macaroni, Aunt Kerry arrived to take Wes to another doctor's appointment. She greeted the girls with a warm wave from the porch that led to the driveway. Together, the girls listened as Wes moseyed out and said, "Really unseasonably cold today, isn't it? Did you see her in there? My Lola is here from her internship."

"I think you mean Audrey, Wes," Aunt Kerry returned, giving her brother a frown.

There it was. The straw that broke the camel's back. Immediately, Audrey's face scrunched up with sadness, and she burst into volatile tears. Christine, seated next to Audrey, could do nothing but place her hand on Audrey's upper-back and whisper, "It's going to be okay," even though she knew, in matters like this, that wasn't entirely true.

"Tell us what happened," Lola said suddenly. She swept her hand over Audrey's, across the table, and squeezed hard. Her eyes were urgent, with the need to know what happened to her only daughter.

"I just feel so stupid," Audrey said through sputtered gasps. "I don't know. He was...he's this journalist at the newspaper. I thought we were in love."

Christine's heart sank. She remembered being nineteen, in love with someone much older and coming to the understanding that she had just been his plaything. It hadn't been real for him.

"Did you tell him you were pregnant?" Susan asked.

Audrey nodded so that her ponytail flipped around. "He said to get rid of it. I told him no way. I would never. I just..." She dropped her hands to her stomach and glanced down at the flat palms. It was difficult to imagine her as a voluptuous pregnant woman, as she still looked like a beautiful young teenaged girl.

Susan's eyes burned toward Christine as Audrey shook with more tears. Christine gulped back the rest of her wine and stood to walk back into the house. Susan followed. Inside, she drew her arms over her chest and said, "I think we should give them some space."

From the living area, they could hear Lola muttering, "I thought we'd been over this a million times. I thought you were using protection. I thought you understood..."

"Mom! I know! You don't have to lecture me. The deed has already been done," Audrey cried.

"Maybe you're right," Christine agreed. "Poor girl."

Christine and Susan grabbed their purses and headed to one of the Inn cars. Christine jumped in the driver's seat, while Susan sat slowly, gazing at something on her phone.

"What is it?" Christine asked.

"Just Amanda. She wants help with something to do with the wedding," she said.

Christine couldn't help it: she snorted. Susan gave her another dirty look.

"What?" Christine demanded.

"You don't have to pretend it isn't hard for you," Susan said, turning to look at her little sister.

"I don't know what you mean," Christine said. She cranked the engine and shot them out of the driveway toward Edgartown. Had Susan really just brought up the lingering feeling Christine had in her gut all the time? The shame and sadness that she wasn't a mother and couldn't have kids?

Christine parked the car near Felix Neck, and the two of them hiked for a bit, walking slowly and avoiding conversation at all costs. When enough time had passed, they returned to the car. Christine had an idea.

"Where are we going?" Susan finally asked, shoving her phone into her purse and drawing one leg over the other.

"You'll see," Christine offered.

It was just after four-thirty in the afternoon, which meant the Edgartown Bar had probably only just opened. Stan Ellis was certainly the kind of guy to get there as early as possible—drink himself to death before eight or nine at night and then stumble back to wherever it was he laid his head every night. As Susan and Christine stood outside, looking at the old building, Susan coughed.

"You don't expect me to go in there, do you?" she asked.

"This is where he hangs out," Christine said.

"And you just want to accost him? Right here?" Susan asked.

"I don't know any other way to corner him," Christine returned.

Again, however, the bar was empty except for a few other stragglers. Rita, the bartender, stood in a dark blue jumpsuit at the front of the bar, near a television that glowed. She seemed focused on a TV game show, a rerun from probably thirty years before.

"It's like stepping back in time," Susan murmured.

Christine ordered them both white wines, and they padded

toward the back of the bar again. She pointed out the various photographs taken of Stan Ellis from the era when he and their mother had fallen in love. Susan's eyes glittered mysteriously as she looked at them.

"I don't like it here," Susan said slowly.

"Let's just sit down."

They did. Susan seemed willing to do anything to avoid Christine's eye contact. For this reason, Christine drank a little too quickly, having to buy herself another round when Susan wasn't even half-way finished her first. When she sat back down, Susan's eyes blared into her.

"You would tell me if it has become a problem, right?" Susan asked, eyeing Christine's glass of wine.

Christine's nostrils flared. "What are you talking about?"

"Your drinking. You'd tell me if you need help, right?"

"You're going to do this here? In the middle of the Edgartown Bar?" Christine demanded. Anger rose up like a wave and crumpled against her heart.

Susan shook her head and muttered something, words Christine's ears couldn't articulate. Christine suddenly wanted to curse this day. It had started out so beautifully, so alive—a pastry chef position, and her beautiful niece's arrival. Now, she and her sister sat in a bar, struggling to relate to one another while her younger sister drilled her daughter about her first pregnancy.

Perhaps this was the reality, though. Susan and Lola knew Christine through-and-through. And Christine couldn't run from the truth of herself.

But Susan surprised her.

"I just can't stop thinking about that poor girl at home," she said. "She wants to be a journalist so bad. She wants to please Lola. You can see it and they only had each other for years and now, everything has fallen apart. I wish I could think of a way to help her."

"At nineteen, we had to figure out everything ourselves," Christine said.

"But we shouldn't have had to," Susan whispered.

Suddenly, Rita switched the song on the stereo. Billy Joel's "Uptown Girl" ripped through the speakers, shifting the mood in the bar to a more upbeat one. As she cleaned the bar counter, Rita tossed her shoulders to-and-fro in line with the music. Susan and Christine found themselves doing it, too.

"Mom loved this song," Susan said suddenly, her smile wide.

"She used to strut around the house, singing it while cleaning," Christine said.

Susan knocked her wine glass back and ordered another. The mood had changed considerably between them. Slowly, Susan began to tell Christine things about her newfound life on Martha's Vineyard—things Christine wouldn't have known just through observation.

Like, "Scott is actually a better kisser now than he was before," which made Christine double-over with laughter.

"I mean, I should hope so! He's had a lot more years to practice," she said.

"Oh, you. I mean, you've been out there, playing the field for years. I didn't know what I was missing with Richard. He was such a snore. Sometimes, I pity that Penelope girl. She's thirty-one, and she wants to marry a man whose idea of a good time is Scrabble and lights out at nine-thirty."

Christine snorted. "I wish I would have met him more than just that one time. He looked so handsome in the wedding photos you sent. I put them on whatever fridge I had back then, but my roommate took them off. He said he didn't believe in marriage. I wonder if Dad had them up anywhere? Gosh. I just really wish I could have gone. How strange that Lola and I missed our sister's only wedding."

Susan bit hard on her lower lip. Christine realized she'd pushed the mood back down. Flustered, she searched her mind for something else to say, something to make her laugh.

"Besides. Penelope and Richard don't know what you're up to on the daily," she began, imitating Susan's marijuana pen near her lips. "You're a wildflower child."

Susan's face fell completely. She looked as though she had seen a ghost. "Will you stop bringing that up?"

"Why? I love that you're into weed," Christine said, with a strange, guttural laugh. "It's just completely off-brand, which makes me love it all the more."

"You just really don't know what you're talking about," Susan returned.

For a moment, Christine thought that Susan might bolt from her chair and storm out of the bar. She held her breath, waiting. Of course, Susan wasn't that type of person. Patience flung over her as she nodded, turning her eyes to the ground.

"Anyway. I'll buy us another round if you get Rita to play another Billy Joel song. I think I'm starting to like it here, as weird as that sounds," Susan said.

Christine ordered them another two glasses of wine, as Rita switched the song to "Scenes from an Italian Restaurant," which kept the girls singing and dancing for a little while longer. Christine and Susan had hardly any memories together like this: just the two of them, exchanging secrets, and finding common ground. Christine was so grateful for it. She was so happy they'd been able to try again.

CHAPTER 13

SEVERAL DAYS LATER, CHRISTINE FINISHED UP THE PASTRY baking for the morning and moseyed toward the front lobby of the Inn, bleary-eyed but happy. Susan and Scott stood in front of the desk, as Scott spoke to someone on the phone.

"Yes. Thank you for letting us know, officer," he said.

"What's up?" Christine asked as he hung up.

"They almost got Chuck again, in Vermont this time," he said. He heaved a sigh and then collected his arms around Susan. "They want us to come up to the mainland to look at some paperwork."

"But we'll be back tomorrow or the next day at the latest," Susan affirmed. She dotted the sides of her eyes with a handkerchief.

Was it possible that Susan and Scott were really so emotional about Chuck Frampton's disappearance? Something about it didn't stack up.

"Looks like the bistro's getting a heavy lunch rush," Susan said suddenly, breaking the hug and nodding. Outside, a gorgeous Porsche flew up toward the side of the Inn. A driver bustled out and then opened the back passenger door to reveal a gorgeous blonde in long, elegant Louboutin heels and what looked like a thousand-dollar sundress.

Christine hustled toward the window of the lobby to watch as the woman walked toward the bistro, her shoulders whipped back and her long legs drawing out before her like she walked a catwalk. Christine's heart thudded. She would have recognized that woman anywhere.

"It's Cheryl Donahue. The editor for Bon Appetit magazine," she whispered, mostly to herself.

When she turned back around, she found Scott and Susan both displaying lackluster smiles. It was obvious they were from very different worlds.

"Don't you get it?" Christine demanded, looking at both of them. "Zach is going to be in over his head. When she visited us at Chez Frank, one of our waiters passed out from stress."

Before they could answer, Christine flung herself back down the hallway that led toward the bistro. Just before Cheryl entered the bistro, she tossed herself into the kitchen and gave Zach a huge, bug-eyed look.

"You had better buckle up, Zach Walters. You're about to be on the ride of your life," she told him.

It didn't take long to explain. After all, Cheryl Donahue was something of a god-like name for those in the industry. Still, Zach sprang into action, muttering to himself as he did his work.

"Is this really what we're going to give Cheryl Donahue? Does it really represent the bistro exactly right? Ronnie! Come here.

Only give her this wine list, not the other one," he said. His words were almost frantic. "And be charming, but not overly so. She doesn't like a brownnoser. Oh, and Ronnie..."

Ronnie flung around at the door, all the blood draining from his cheeks.

"This is one of the most important days of your life. But don't stress," Zach said, pointing at him.

When Ronnie disappeared to seat Cheryl and give her the wine list and a fancy bottle of water, Zach pressed his hands against the sterling counter. He looked on the verge of a panic attack.

"Let me stay and help out," Christine said suddenly.

"What? No. You've been here since four in the morning," Zach said.

"Come on, Zach. I'm used to this from Chez Frank. I'll be your right-hand man," Christine said. She grabbed an apron and, in no time, began to prep vegetables and banter with Zach about the appropriate dishes to reveal to Cheryl.

They decided on the walnut and endive and goat cheese salad for a starter, along with a basket of Christine's freshly-baked croissants, which she would surely pick at but not eat fully. Afterward, they would serve fish and a pasta course, along with the crowning jewel of Christine's dessert-making abilities: the crème brûlée.

"When I made it for her at Chez Frank, she nearly swooned," Christine said.

"You're my secret weapon," Zach said as he hurriedly rushed about the kitchen,

Zach and Christine fell into a familiar rhythm, as Ronnie bucked in and out to serve dish after dish. After the fish was taken out, Christine and Zach hovered just outside the window of the kitchen to watch as Cheryl took her first, contemplative bite, nodded with her eyes closed, and then made a little note to herself on her napkin.

"Is that a good sign?" Zach demanded. "I can't tell."

"Nobody can tell with her," Christine returned.

After she had prepared the crème brûlée, Christine marched out with the little dish and hovered over Cheryl's table with the fire blower. This was a skill she'd mastered nearly twenty years before, something that had given her ultimate power over some of the other men in her pastry and culinary classes. She wasn't afraid. As she placed the piping hot dish in front of Cheryl, the woman muttered, "My goodness. Just as good as I might find in Manhattan. How splendid."

Twenty minutes later, three-quarters of her crème brûlée was finished, and the last of her sparkling wine danced at the bottom of her wine glass, Cheryl rose and marched toward the kitchen. At the entrance, hovering just a few feet from where Zach and Christine stood, both in shock, she called, "I would like to take your photographs, you two. I've not had such a splendid meal on Martha's Vineyard in years."

Christine and Zach shared a panicked, yet pleased look, before joining Cheryl in the main dining room. Cheryl delivered no more compliments after this, but posed with them, with a large gorgeous smile, and then immediately got on her phone to tell her secretary she would have the article written in three days' time. Christine and Zach watched as the woman clacked out in her Louboutin heels and then disappeared into the afternoon summer air. The moment she retreated into her Porsche, Christine and Zach fell into each other's arms and hopped around, making themselves out to be absolute fools to the rest of the guests. But they didn't care one bit.

Back in the kitchen, Zach poured them both full glasses of wine and wiped a bead of sweat from his forehead.

"I think if you hadn't come running back into this kitchen to help, I might have died today," he said.

"I know you would have died. I don't want that kind of blood on my hands," Christine said.

They clinked glasses and studied one another through their first sip. Christine pressed her lips together, stirring in panic. What the hell was going on between them? Why did she feel butterflies in her belly and want to kiss him, have him hold her in his strong arms?

All those years ago, she had thought she'd wanted him, too, until he had wronged her.

Why would he be any different now?

"You've been such a surprise, Christine," he said, suddenly snapping her out of her reverie.

Again, her heart thudded.

"I mean, I know you hate me more than the devil himself, but you're also a kind and generous friend when you want to be. I can't thank you enough," Zach said.

The kitchen was empty around them. Ronnie and the other servers were out on the floor, swarming the tables and picking up plates post-lunch-rush. Suddenly, Zach stepped forward and kissed her. His soft lips fell over hers, and her eyes closed, for only a split-second, as her stomach twisted with desire.

No.

The word rang through her and forced her lips away. She

peered up, anxiously into Zach's eyes, knowing she owed him an explanation. But she couldn't give him one. She dropped her wine glass on the counter, grabbed her purse, and rushed from the kitchen. Every part of her body felt like it was on fire.

She wasn't the person Zach Walters wanted her to be. Heck, she wasn't even the type of person she wanted to be. She was a woman that couldn't bear children, a depressed human being, and she felt she could be nothing else. She'd left Frank, her last chance at love, and she wanted nothing to do with horrible heartaches or hopeful plans that usually busted into flames.

By the time she slowed down her run, she was nearly home. She gasped and grabbed her knees as her head pounded. Only a few days into her dream job, and she had messed everything up.

This was oh-so-typical Christine.

CHAPTER 14

W<small>HEN</small> C<small>HRISTINE</small> <small>ENTERED</small> <small>THE</small> <small>MAIN</small> <small>HOUSE,</small> L<small>OLA</small> <small>AND</small> Audrey were in the midst of a blow-out. They stood out on the porch that overlooked the water, facing one another, so that Christine could see the gorgeous outlines of their profiles— matching facial features including their beautiful long dark hair. Even their voices had a similar ring to it. Although the only difference was that Christine could hear the hard-edge to Lola's voice.

"The world of journalism is completely different now than it was in the late-'90s," Lola spewed. "You needed to use this internship to jump off to the next opportunity. You said you wanted to get a middle-editor position at the paper this year, and..."

"Well, I'm guessing they won't want an editor who's six weeks pregnant," Audrey barreled back.

"So you're just going to quit?" Lola demanded.

"I don't know! Mom, why can't you see this from my side and

not from the side of me having failed you, huh?" Audrey asked, not backing down.

Christine's heart fluttered. She stepped deeper into the house, which caused Audrey to shift over and spot her. Her face was etched with so much emotion. Lola cut up to peer through the screen door.

"Sorry about us," Lola said. "We just arrived back from the doctor."

"Got official confirmation of the pregnancy," Audrey said in a mocking tone. "Yay."

Christine stepped out onto the porch. She was bleary-eyed, exhausted, and her lips still buzzed from Zach's kiss.

"I know it's probably not what you want to hear, but someone around here has to wish you congratulations," Christine said suddenly.

Lola's jaw dropped, as Audrey's eyes bugged out of their sockets. Immediately, Christine knew she had said the wrong thing, but how could she say anything different? A baby had been all she had wanted in the world.

"You really don't need to interject your opinion right now, Christine," Lola spat as she started to pace back and forth.

"It's okay, Mom. Come on," Audrey tried. "We are doing this right here in the middle of everything. It's not like we're hiding ourselves."

"No." Lola crossed her arms and glared at Christine. "When you were upstairs a few weeks ago in near-constant drunken fights with Frank over the phone, Susan and I decided that that was your business—that we needed to stay out of your life because we didn't know anything about it. Now, I am asking you for the same respect I gave you."

Christine sputtered. She felt as though she had been punched in the heart. The wind rushed up through the porch and flung her brunette locks back as her tongue stumbled around for something else to say. "For all its negative consequences, having a baby has so, so many benefits and joys, as well. You're picking the girl apart when she only made the same mistake you did at her age."

"She's having a baby with a man who won't even answer his phone when she calls!" Lola cried out.

"Yeah? Well, men are disappointing. I know that. You know that. Women have to be ten times as strong and ten times as optimistic, and we have to lift one another up," Christine continued.

"You can give me this feminist baloney if you want, but you will never understand what it means to be a mother," Lola spewed. "Every single day, I lived for this girl. It was just us. It was only meant to be...."

Suddenly, the screen door whipped open to reveal Wes Sheridan. He looked just as stormy as Lola, his eyes sure of themselves and his lips downturned. He glared at Lola, his hand-stretched over the screen door to hold it open.

"How dare you speak to your sister like that?" he demanded.

Christine fell into an immediate state of shock as the pain of Lola's words cut into her. Nobody spoke for a few moments after that.

"So what, she doesn't have kids. So what? That doesn't mean she isn't a fine and genuine person. That doesn't mean that she isn't worthy of love or compassion."

Lola sputtered. "Dad, you're confused. That isn't what I meant."

"Don't you tell me that I'm confused," Wes stammered. He stepped further out onto the porch, allowing the door to slam closed behind him. "I may be losing my marbles, but I know what I see right in front of me. I see you, Lola, acting like a little brat. I see you, Lola, not understanding how hypocritical you're being with your own damn daughter, Audrey. I'm happier than I've ever been, welcoming you girls back into this house, but if you continue to belittle one another the way you just belittled Christine, then I will have to ask you to leave. Christine loves you. She doesn't deserve that."

With that, Wes turned, grabbed the screen door, and stomped back into the house. Mesmerized, Christine watched him go, while Lola collected her computer and backpack from the porch, glared at Audrey, and said, "We're getting a hotel for the night. Come on."

Audrey's eyes linked with Christine's for a long time as she followed her mother from the porch. Christine felt the fear and pain that swirled there behind those big baby blues. She knew it was a fear she would never fully experience the fear of bringing a life into this world, unsure if you could fully lift it up yourself.

When they were gone, Christine poured herself a glass of wine and snuck onto the porch swing, watching the waves. All her life, she'd imagined her father liked her the least of all the Sheridan sisters. She would have never in a million years written something like what had just occurred. It was enough to make her reconsider her entire life.

Footsteps at the porch door turned Christine's head. Yet again, her father appeared. He looked steadier, less volatile, and he nodded as he approached to sit with her, saying, "I'm sorry I lost my temper earlier. I try not to get so angry, but it seems like it's happening more and more since the diagnosis."

"Hey. You were standing up for me. I can't complain," Christine said.

Wes gave a soft smile. "Ah, poor Lola. She'll figure it all out. She's just so hot-headed. You sometimes have to reel her in when she goes out too far." He finished and gave her arm a pat.

"You must have had different modes of operation for all of our moods," Christine said. "Three teenage girls and no mother. I don't know how you made it through."

"Well, Susan left pretty soon after it all happened," Wes said. "So it was mostly me versus you and Lola. Actually, it was mostly me versus you. I'm sure you remember. You were the hardest teenager in the world to raise."

Christine chuckled. "I'm sorry about that, Dad."

"No need to apologize," Wes said. "I always thought you were the closest in personality to my Anna. You were prone to mood swings and a bit wild sometimes. Always on the verge of something big, if only she was brave enough to go out and get it."

"You've never told me that," Christine marveled, remembering how she had been surprised at her mother's moodiness in the diaries.

"It's difficult, sometimes, to talk about exactly how people were when they were alive, especially if it's not all the cushy, good stuff. Heck, this summer has had that as a theme, hasn't it? Now that you know everything about your mother—about Stan."

Christine blinked down at her half-drunk glass of wine. She felt terribly heavy, as though if she stood, her body might turn to lead and take her down.

"It's a funny thing, isn't it? Both Audrey and Lola are petrified of what will come next, just in case whatever comes next doesn't fulfill whatever it is Lola wants Audrey's life to be. But life doesn't pan out the way we plan it, ever."

"It's like that old expression about the best-laid plans," Wes said, chuckling.

"Exactly. Did I imagine that I would be back on Martha's Vineyard, at age forty-one, drinking myself to death? No," Christine affirmed.

Her father hesitated. Christine knew that she had taken the conversation just a step too far.

"You know you're the most resilient of all of us," Wes said. "I don't know even half of the stories of your life away from here. Susan mentioned you studied for a while in Paris, that you made pastries in Stockholm, that you were one of the most renowned pastry chefs in Manhattan. But I imagine that kind of life, all over the world, brought with it loads of heartache and loneliness," he said.

Christine had never heard her father so articulate. She dropped her head on his shoulder and felt the first of what would surely be many tears, skate toward her cheeks.

"You're a good person, Christine. Remember that you don't have to escape from anything anymore. Not here on the Vineyard. We're here for each other, now. Even Lola, although she did a bad job of showing it today," Wes continued.

Christine let silence stretch between them for a moment. The waves shuffled up against the dock and shifted it this way, then gently back. She wondered where Zach was, what he thought of the kiss they had shared. Surely, the fact that she had run out had been answer enough. She couldn't be anything for anyone except her family—least of all him.

"I love you, Dad," Christine said.

"I love you, too, Christine," her father returned. "At this moment, maybe even slightly more than the other two, but don't tell them that."

Christine laughed at the absurdity of it. Of course, it couldn't be true. But she held her head on his shoulder for a long time as the pair of them watched the afternoon drip by. They were now deep into the tourist season. Always, in this late-July era, there was the inescapable feeling that it was all about to crash down around them and end. Once summer was over, you couldn't get it back. It was never exactly the same.

CHAPTER 15

CHRISTINE AND HER FATHER WENT TO BED JUST AFTER EIGHT in the evening. Although Christine had pondered leaving the bistro altogether, she decided that an early wake-up call of just after three-thirty, alongside an urgent and lonely shift in the bistro kitchen, was the way to go. This way, she could avoid Zach, prepare the pastries and desserts, and make it home for breakfast with her father.

She laid out the perfectly-buttered croissants in the window by the walk-up, then turned back to align the pies and cakes in the display case inside. Just as she prepared to remove her apron, there was a knock at the walk-up window. She blinked to see a line nearly twenty-feet long, all the way toward the docks.

Sunrise Cove Inn Bistro had never had that kind of walk-up traffic before.

Beyond that, it was still only eight in the morning, which meant most of the morning staff wouldn't clock in until eight-thirty at the earliest. Panicked, Christine shot up to the window, prepared to tell them that it wasn't yet time. The moment she did, however, the forty-something woman tourist outside the window flashed her phone around and said, "You won't believe how Cheryl Donahue raved about you on Instagram. I just have to try one of your croissants before I leave the island."

This stopped Christine in her tracks. She hadn't investigated Cheryl's social media channels yet, especially after all the chaos of the previous day, but it was clear, they'd made an impression. In the next fifteen minutes, she sold all the croissants and baked breads and other pastries in the walk-up glass case.

Through the window, she spotted Zach as he parked his truck in the lot next to the Inn. He opened the door and balked at the large line. Immediately after, his eyes connected with Christine's. She gave him a huge shrug and he laughed, loud enough for her to hear it in the bistro. Although she didn't want to spend any time with him, seeing him like this made her heart perform little flips of panic.

"That's all, folks!" Christine said to the rest of the line. "I'll be better prepared tomorrow if you promise to come back. I'm so sorry."

The rest of the line groaned and turned back. Christine was left with a pile of money and a huge grin smeared across her face. When she turned around, she nearly fell directly into Ronnie, who struggled to see out the window.

"Were all those people here for your baked goods?" he asked.

"I guess so," Christine said.

Christine could hear Zach's booming voice just outside the

kitchen. She didn't want to hang around, so she gave Ronnie a tip to clean up the walk-up area, then grabbed her purse and headed out.

Back outside, there was a little skip to her step. The air still felt fresh and vibrant. It hinted at all the possibilities of an early morning, after such a long shift of work.

When Christine arrived back home, she found Wes, Audrey, and Aunt Kerry out on the back porch eating croissants she had brought home the day before. Each held a mug of coffee.

"Hey there!" Aunt Kerry said.

"Hey!" Christine said. "Where's Lola?"

"She got a random call last night asking her to do a story about some writer in Boston," Audrey said. "She didn't want to pass it up, so she caught the early ferry this morning. She'll be back tomorrow."

Christine sat with everyone for a while. Wes and Aunt Kerry discussed Charlotte, who had lost her husband in a boating accident the year before and now struggled with bouts of depression. Wes's eyes burned toward Christine's. She was grateful that now, he understood the weight of her inner emotional struggles. It felt incredible to have such honesty with her father.

Around noon, Aunt Kerry and Wes decided to head to town for lunch and a card game with some of their friends from high school. This left Audrey and Christine alone at the house together for the first time ever.

Perhaps on a different day, this would have made Christine panicked, especially given what had happened between Audrey and Christine and Lola the day before. But today? She was still high off her kiss with Zach Walters. Her croissants were Vineyard-famous and she refused to fall into the depths of sadness once again.

"Why don't we borrow Scott's boat?" she heard herself ask Audrey.

Audrey blinked those big eyes up from her phone. At first, Christine thought she would say she was busy or tired, but she surprised her and said, "Yeah, sure. Let me change into my suit."

Since Scott and Susan were still off the island, Christine texted real quick to make sure Scott was cool with them using it. Susan texted back immediately that it was fine and to have fun. After all, Scott had left the boat docked at the Sheridan residence for just this purpose.

Just before Audrey arrived downstairs, Christine made them turkey and cheddar sandwiches on homemade bread, grabbed a spare bag of chips, and, pointedly, left the wine at home. Audrey couldn't drink at nineteen and pregnant, and she didn't want to drink in front of her niece anyway. She wanted to spend some much-needed quality time to get to know her better.

Down in the speed boat, Christine revved the engine, making the boat shake beneath her. Audrey walked down the dock in only a red two-piece swimming suit. It was hard to believe there was any kind of being in that stomach. It looked as though she couldn't even fit a sandwich in there.

"You know how to drive this thing?" Audrey said with a laugh as she hopped on.

"Oh, yeah. Growing up on the Vineyard, you kind of have to know this stuff," Christine returned. "Dad would have felt he failed us as a father if we didn't know."

They chugged out onto the open Vineyard Sound on the

northwestern part of the island, between Martha's Vineyard and Naushon Island, and eased about a half-mile away from Makonikey. Christine pointed out the various places she remembered, including Cedar Tree Neck Sanctuary. "There's a great beach over there. North Shore," she said. "I had a few wild nights there if you can believe it. I know to you it must feel like I'm a million years old, though."

Audrey rolled her eyes. "No way. You and Mom and Aunt Susan all seem so young. I'll be grateful if I look anything like you guys later."

Christine laughed. There was a strange pause. Christine's thoughts raced to the ideas of Audrey's child. Would she have a daughter? A fourth generation of Sheridan women?

"Thanks for what you said yesterday to Mom," Audrey said suddenly. She ripped open a bag of chips and peered into it contemplatively before grabbing one single salty crisp and placing it on her tongue.

"I don't know if I said the right thing or not," Christine said. She gripped the steering wheel and sat at the edge of the driver's seat with her athletic legs flung out before her, in the splendor of the sun. "But I know it must be so stressful for both of you in really different ways."

Audrey nodded. "I mean, I agree with her about almost all of it. That's the hardest part. I do want a journalism career. I do want to get the top jobs at the New York Times or The Tribune or LA Times. I don't want to be glanced over because I already have a kid. I was a complete idiot. He wants me to deal with it, I just..."

"I understand," Christine murmured, although, how could she?

Audrey dropped her head further back on the seat rest and stared at the beautiful blue sky. She looked like a painting of youthful longing.

"Like, do you think when I have this baby, I will look at it every day and blame it for everything that's wrong with my life?" Audrey asked with a fear in her eyes that made Christine almost flinch.

"I don't think it's possible to feel that way about your baby," Christine assured her as best she could.

"I don't think so, either. I asked Mom last night at the hotel if she thought that way about me. She said no, but that it was different. She didn't want anything really until after I was born. Apparently, my birth made her want to become something."

"Babies can do a lot of things, but I think, generally, they normally do good in this world," Christine offered. "They're a bit of hope."

"That's what I think, too."

Audrey and Christine unwrapped their sandwiches. Before Audrey took a bite, she said, "I hate that I never knew you guys growing up. I used to ask Mom about it, and she just said, she wasn't a family person anymore. I guess that's all changed."

"Like the drop of a hat," Christine said with a laugh.

"I'm happy it worked out that way. Mom seems different. At least, she did, before all this happened. Ugh. Making that phone call that day to tell her that I had messed everything up? It was one of the worst days of my life."

"I've had a lot of bad days. Trust me. You're doing okay for yourself," Christine said.

Audrey chuckled and opened her fingers so that she could peer between them. "Tell me."

So, Christine told her a few stories of her shadowed past. She told her about the French boyfriend she'd had during her stint in Paris who had cheated on her with an Italian model. She told her about the first apartment she'd had to herself in Brooklyn, where rats had infested the first floor and forced them all out on the street for a full week. "I stayed at a crummy hostel because I hardly knew anyone in the city at the time," Christine confessed. "Until, of course, I slept with one of my culinary school professors and stayed with him for a few days."

"Oh, my gosh, Aunt Christine!" Audrey said. She grinned madly. "I knew you've had a wild life, but I didn't know the details. I think my mom was jealous of that—of you not having kids."

This surprised Christine. Immediately, Audrey backtracked and said, "I mean, don't get me wrong; she loves me. But she wanted to live in New York and Paris and wherever else you lived, just for the stories. And she had to keep things kind of stable because of me."

As she spoke, Audrey's face grew more and more shadowed. She bit down on her lower lip and then stretched her arm down to drip her fingers through the light waves. "I guess I've trapped myself, too."

Christine furrowed her brow and listened as the waves lapped against the boat, rocking it. Finally, she said, "You know, I lost my chance to have a baby."

Immediately, Audrey tore her head toward Christine, her eyes wide in shock. "What? I just thought that you didn't want any."

Christine shook her head, vehemently. "Not true at all. I wanted to be a mother almost more than anything in the world. But there was something wrong with my ovary, and I had to get it taken out about six years ago. Your Aunt Susan came up to New York to help me through it. It was one of the worst moments of my life. After that, a lot of the guys I dated always dated me with an asterisk. They knew I couldn't have their kids. I wasn't a real option. I lived in one of the most beautiful metropolitan cities in the world, and still, all the old rules of Martha's Vineyard applied. I didn't matter to them."

Audrey's eyes glowed with tears. "You're saying there's never a right time for anything, aren't you?"

Christine nodded, adding an ironic laugh. "Being a woman is the toughest thing in the world. I swear every woman I know is five times stronger than any man."

Suddenly, Audrey stood and rushed toward Christine and hugged her hard, making the boat rip to-and-fro. Christine felt overwhelmed with emotion. Whatever this was, it felt akin to a love from a child to a mother. She had never had anything like that before. There, they hugged beneath the gorgeous eggshell blue sky, surrounded by the chaos of the Vineyard Sound, the same water that had swallowed up her mother and never given her back.

CHAPTER 16

T‍HE NEXT MORNING, C‍HRISTINE ROSE EARLY TO PERFORM THE same duties she had done the previous day. Luckily, Ronnie arrived at seven-thirty to help her with the last of it and man the back walk-up window. When Christine asked him about it, he shrugged and said Zach had asked if he could come in to help. This could have been taken one of two ways, Christine reasoned. One, Zach wanted to keep a distance between himself and Christine just as much as she did, or two, Zach just wanted to relieve her after a hard several-hour shift.

Back at the house, Christine found Lola, Scott, Susan, Wes, and Audrey on the back porch. As she entered, Audrey finished up her story about the previous afternoon with Christine on the Sound. Lola's eyes turned toward Christine's. She seemed both surprised and a bit upset, as though Christine wasn't allowed this spare time alone with her niece. Still, regardless of Lola's apparent jealousy, Christine wouldn't have traded that memory for the world.

"Sounds like you guys had a beautiful day," Susan said. "Was it strange to be back at the wheel of the boat?"

"Not really," Christine said. "I guess I was never really a city girl, after all. How did it go with the police?"

Susan and Scott exchanged a glance. Again, Christine found it very difficult to decipher, like they had created a language all their own.

"It was okay," Susan finally sputtered. "There's still no sign of exactly where he went, but they're on the hunt."

"He's kind of an old-fashioned guy, so modern techniques don't work so well with him," Scott affirmed.

"And your story, Lola?" Christine asked.

"Oh? Just another stuck-up writer with a lot of stories to tell," Lola said with a laugh. "Of course, he has every reason to be stuck-up. It was some of the better stuff I've read in years."

"So you don't have to fake the story," Audrey said. "Make him seem more important than he is."

"Thankfully," Lola said.

"I had to do that last year at the paper," Audrey said. "This man who did sculptures—his entire masterpiece fell apart right before the art show. He tried to make it seem like it had all been on purpose. I forgot exactly what he said in the interview, something about how it was meant to reflect the loose nature of time or something."

Susan and Christine laughed, while Wes blinked at all of them in confusion. Lola, of course, grimaced. Everyone knew what was on her mind. She didn't want to be reminded that Audrey's current journalism career was over.

"We have to go up to Boston," Susan suddenly interjected, maybe as a means to take everyone's mind off Lola's anger. "Tomorrow."

"Oh? Why?" Christine asked.

Again, Susan seemed cagey. "There's more to go over with the case. You know how I am with all of this—a bit obsessive."

"I would probably just leave it all alone if it weren't for her," Scott said, his words coming a bit too quickly.

"You really need to explain to me how all this goes," Audrey said. "I'm fascinated with your career, Aunt Susie."

"I'll definitely chat with you about some of my strangest cases when I have more time," Susan said.

"Just a hint! I can hardly take it!" Audrey said.

"Hmmm. There was the college kid who kidnapped his girlfriend and kept her in a cabin in the woods..." Susan said, her eyes sparkling.

"No! I read about that when it happened! That was your client?" Audrey cried.

"Oh, yes. Good kid. He always asked for grape soda when we met together," Susan said.

"Good kid?" Christine asked with a laugh.

Susan shrugged. "I mean, in the context of the other people I worked with, sure. Always flossed his teeth."

Aunt Kerry arrived a few minutes later with a large vat of her famous clam chowder. Christine hadn't expected this, and it seemed nobody else had either, but nobody was in any mood to turn it down. They sat out on the porch and dipped their spoons into the liquid goodness and laughed throughout the rest of the afternoon. At one point, Lola grabbed a bottle of wine from the kitchen and asked Christine if she wanted a glass. She surprised herself with her answer.

"Not right now, thanks. Maybe later."

After lunch, Wes laid down for a nap; Aunt Kerry went back to Uncle Trevor, who, she said, was in the middle of a big fight with the lawnmower and Lola headed into town for a drink with an old high school friend. Susan and Scott excused themselves for a boat ride. This left Audrey and Christine together again. As they shared casual banter and laughed, they cleared the picnic table and scrubbed up the dishes in the kitchen. Audrey paused and looked up at the framed picture of Wes and Anna from circa 1977, when Anna had been around twenty-two years old.

"It's really eerie. It's like looking into a mirror," Audrey said.

"Mom's genes must be so strong. They beat out Dad's in every way possible," Christine said, letting out a little laugh.

"When I met Susan's daughter, Amanda, on the ferry a few weeks ago, I felt exactly the same way," Audrey said. "You know, I think it's insanely selfish of both Mom and Aunt Susan that Amanda and I were never able to hang out. It's not like we were that far away."

Christine sighed and dabbed a towel across her hands. "It's complicated, I guess."

Audrey swallowed. "Do you get the sense that Susan and Scott are lying about something?"

Christine was surprised enough to answer honestly. "Actually, I do."

"What do you think it could be?" Audrey asked.

"I have no idea. Even since I got back to the Vineyard, Susan has felt like she's drifted further and further away from me. I thought I would return to my sisters and that we would build our relationships even more, but I don't know. I guess I was wrong again." She bit her lower lip, hating that she'd already said so much. Audrey didn't deserve to be in the middle of all that.

"Should we ask Aunt Susan about it?" Audrey tried. "Just point-blank. Surprise her into telling us what's up. It can't all be about Chuck."

There was a creak on the steps. Audrey and Christine turned to find Wes, rubbing at one eye and giving them a sleepy smile.

"Oh, no! Did we wake you?" Christine asked.

"No, no. I can't get much of a good nap in. I always wake up and think I'm wasting so much time of my life! Besides, I wanted to ask you, girls, if you wanted to head to the beach with me," Wes said.

It was decided they would head off to the west, back toward Aquinnah Cliffs Overlook, so that Audrey could see it for the first time. As he snapped his seat belt across his waist in the passenger seat, Wes said he hadn't been to the cliffs in ages.

"Anna used to love it over there," he said wistfully.

"We went there so many times as children," Christine said as she cranked the engine.

"Gosh, you're lucky. All I did as a kid was go to the Dairy Queen," Audrey said with a laugh.

As they headed west, Christine stopped at a little market to pick up a few items for a later snack. Clouds billowed up across the blue sky, making it textured and more alive than its normal, cerulean self. By the time they reached the cliffs, a slight rain had begun to patter across the glass.

"Shoot," Christine said, gripping the steering wheel as they sat in the parking lot. "I guess we should have checked the forecast."

"It's only a sprinkle," Wes said. He pressed against the door, opened it, and immediately shot out toward the edge of the cliffs.

Audrey and Christine exchanged glances, shrugged, then followed after him. After the mugginess in the air, the light rain felt incredible, cooling. Together, they hovered over the edge of the cliffs and gazed down at the monstrous waves, which tossed against the clay rocks.

"It's gorgeous," Audrey murmured.

"When I was a boy, I used to stand right here in this spot and throw rock after rock down there," Wes said, trying to take another safe peak over the cliff.

Throughout the afternoon and into the evening, Wes, Audrey, and Christine walked along the edge of the rocks, eased down toward the beach, and dipped in and out of the water as they pleased. As the sun began to sink lower toward the horizon, threatening to deliver them into the night, the three sat on spare towels they had found in the car and watched as the ocean turned from orange to pink to purple. It was pure poetry.

"I think you're doing the right thing, Audrey," Wes said suddenly.

The words were surprising. Audrey and Christine blinked toward him, waiting.

"I know your mom thinks you've messed up. But I would never think of it that way," he said. "We in the Sheridan clan have so, so much love to give. Back when I first had my girls, I was almost overwhelmed with the amount of love I felt for them. For my Anna, my Susan, my Christine, and my Lola. Time passes quickly. And I don't know that I can say I'll always have the memories. But I don't regret a single thing."

Audrey's eyes shimmered with tears. Christine wrapped an arm around her shoulders, pulling her in closer.

"Thank you, Grandpa," Audrey murmured. "It means a lot to hear you say that."

"But that should go for you, too, Christine," he continued.

Christine arched her brow in confusion.

"You have just as much love to give as the rest of us, and you're just as deserving of love, too," Wes continued.

Christine guffawed as Wes tapped the side of his nose.

"I know you better than you think I do," he said with a sneaky smile. "I think I know what's going on in that cranium of yours. You think the story is over because you came back. But it's only just begun."

CHAPTER 17

CHRISTINE PONDERED HER DAD'S WORDS THROUGHOUT THE night, staring up into the blackness. Every few seconds, her stomach stabbed and panged with the memory of Zach's kiss. The way he had looked at her had nothing to do with their stupid high school feud and everything to do with two adults with similar interests, and a lot of love in their hearts.

Maybe all the chaos they had put themselves through back in high school had only been leading them to this moment. Maybe, like Susan, she could find happiness on the island she'd run away from so many years ago. Maybe this was her forever.

She awoke with a level of optimism she hardly recognized in herself. On a kind of mission, she folded the croissants and baked the cakes and stirred up frosting, her hands moving like butterflies over the batter. By the time Ronnie arrived to help at the walk-up counter, she had worked herself up into a tizzy.

"Zach's off today," Ronnie said, almost immediately, as he

bagged croissants for eager tourists. "He takes one day off every two weeks. What do you think he does with his time off? Me and the other busboy have a bet going."

Christine laughed. "What do you think he's up to?"

"Well, he's pretty obsessed with fine dining and really good at making delicious food," Ronnie said. "So my bet is that he just surrounds himself with fast food, anything disgusting and sugary from his childhood, and just vegs out all day. If he spends his whole life committed to only good quality things, he'll go nuts."

Christine was disappointed that Zach had made an appearance, but she wasn't deterred. She headed into Zach's office, with an excuse to leave him a note, and found on a spare envelope the address of Zach's actual house in Edgartown.

Sensing that eight in the morning wasn't a good time to head to Edgartown—especially not on his only day to sleep in, she spent the morning and early afternoon on the Joseph Sylvia State beach, attempting to read but continually falling into daydreams, all of which revolved around some kind of cushy future she and Zach could create together.

"No, I can't have children," she heard herself telling a future Zach, "But that doesn't mean we can't be happy. There are so many options for us. And besides. Isn't the bistro kind of like our baby?"

When it came time to go to Edgartown, her thoughts had reached an intense and loud pitch. As she drove toward his place, she whispered to herself, her eyes feeling on the verge of burning holes in the road.

"Calm down, Christine," she muttered to herself. "You're just going to talk to him. You don't have to do anything brash. You don't have to hold a boom box over your head and tell him you think you're soul mates."

She had never done anything like this before. With other guys, she had gotten together with them after drunken nights, drunken accidents--stuff they had decided to try just because of their dark and sometimes silly decisions.

Zach's house was located near the waterline. It was a stony cottage with a low roof and a little porch that looked out toward the eastern-island waves. Christine parked the car along the road and peered up, her heart bumping in her throat. This was the craziest thing she had ever done, maybe--or the most genuine. Maybe both. She wasn't sure.

Christine clutched the bag of fresh croissants she had packed, a gift, and used her other hand to rap on the door. Two voices vibrated on the other side before Zach appeared, wearing a pair of jeans and a black v-neck. His smile was plastic-like and difficult to read.

"Christine. Hey. What's up?"

He had never spoken to her like this, so stoically as though they were strangers. It was obvious that she had done the wrong thing, coming over like this, unannounced. She felt it like a rock in her stomach. Seconds later, a woman appeared a few feet behind Zach. There was a strange pause.

"Remy, this is Christine. She's the new pastry chef at the bistro," Zach said. His voice was strained.

Christine lifted her hand warily. Remy did the same as she stepped forward. Up close, Christine recognized that she had recently been crying; her eyes were lined with red.

"Remy is someone I met at culinary school in Boston," he said.

"Oh," Christine said.

She felt as though she was at the top of the water, peering down below the surface, unable to see more than a foot or two deep.

Why had she come here again? To tell him she was falling in love with him?

Right. How stupid.

It had all been a mistake.

"Well, I just came to drop these off," Christine said. "Like we talked about before—a new recipe." Christine shoved the bag of croissants toward Zach, forcing him to take them. "I'm still pretty new at the bistro and I just want to make sure I'm, you know, making all the right choices," she tried to explain, her eyes on Remy.

Remy was really, particularly beautiful. She was a red-headed thin and short little thing, maybe one hundred and ten pounds and in her late-thirties. Maybe she had come to the Vineyard to retry what they'd had before. Maybe she'd come to the Vineyard to do exactly what Christine had planned to do now.

Thank goodness, she wouldn't have the opportunity to tell him. She could lock that side of her heart away for good and, of course, throw away the key. The kiss had obviously meant nothing to him. It was just as well.

"Well, I'm off, then," Christine said. "Thanks again, Zach, and I guess I'll talk to you at the bistro. Yep. Okay, see you."

With that, she spun around and shuffled down off the porch and back toward her car. She hardly allowed herself a single thought, a single frantic fear, until she yanked up in front of the Edgartown Bar again, unclear, totally, how she had even gotten there.

Why on earth had she returned to the Vineyard? Had she really assumed that she would be able to rebuild whatever happiness she'd had as a kid? Heck, whatever that happiness had been, it was all an illusion, anyway. She'd always been the one with so much angst. She'd always had a heart of black.

And when she'd actually thought Zach Walters was into her in high school, he had made himself very clear and ripped her heart in two.

This was no different.

He had just wanted to get back at her, maybe or prove just how much better he was, even though she had worked her way up through the culinary world. No matter how far you got in this life, there was always someone there, ready to tug you back down.

She snapped out of her reverie while standing at the bar counter. Rita blinked at her and said, "I'm going to ask you again. What do you want to drink?"

"Right. I'm sorry," Christine whispered. "I want a vodka tonic. Please."

It was not time for a vodka tonic. It was barely four-thirty in the afternoon. But in minutes, Christine found herself staring straight ahead, both hands gripping her chilled vodka tonic, listening to Rita's game shows blare on and on. When her eyes cleared again, she realized she stared directly at one of the photographs of Stan Ellis.

Stan Ellis. The man who had started it all—who had decimated her family.

Suddenly, Christine marched back up to Rita. Rita gave her a confused smile, one that seemed to say, *Please, stop interrupting my TV show.*

"What can I do for you now, honey?" she asked.

"I wondered if you could tell me where Stan Ellis lives?" Christine said.

Rita arched one of her overly plucked brows. "What is this about?"

"It's really important," Christine said. "I'm leaving the Vineyard for good tomorrow, and I need to talk to him before I go back to New York. You must know that he was a good friend of my mother's."

This was the only card Christine could play. While Lola dealt with her Audrey debacle, and Scott and Susan brewed in their own secrets, Christine wanted one thing and one thing only: to face the man who had killed her mother, tell him just what she thought of him, and then return to New York.

It had never been right to come back here. It had been little more than a vacation. That was all. When she thought of it in a year or two, when she was surely back on her feet as a pastry chef in another restaurant in Manhattan, it would be just a blip in her memories.

Rita studied her for a long time. Finally, she said, "You promise he'll be all right if I give you his address?"

"More than all right. I think it's about time the two of us have some kind of conversation is all," Christine said, holding her stare.

Rita scribbled an address on the back of an old envelope and passed it her way. "It's at the very far end of this road," she said. "When you think you've gone too far, you've still got about a half-mile to go. He's along the water. You'll see his boat tied to the dock below. I'm sure you've seen his boat before."

"Anywhere you go on this island, you see Stan Ellis out fishing," Christine returned.

"That's what I thought," Rita said.

Christine took the envelope, paid her bill, and raced back to the car. Her heart had moved fully into her throat and banged away in there. After accosting Zach, it was time to accost Stan. Then, she would get off the island as quickly as she could, taking Felix, who would probably miss the warm embrace of her father along with her, and start a new life. Maybe in Queens—she'd never tried Queens.

Rita had been right about the route to Stan's. Christine snuck the car onto a gravel road and bumped along, moving just about five miles an hour, glancing left and right at each of the little shacks that led down toward the Sound. Just when she had thought she had gone too far, she pushed herself forward, until a crooked shack that reminded her of Scott's little house, popped up next to a little cliffside. She stopped the car and blinked at it.

So this was it. This was the life her mother had wanted to abandon them for.

Christine held her breath as she stepped up the rickety staircase. The windows were dark, shadowed, but Stan's boat clacked against the dock down below the house. This meant there was a good chance he was around.

Christine lifted her hand and rapped it delicately against the door. The sound echoed through what looked like three rooms: a kitchen, which held a little table and a single chair, a living area with an old TV, and a bedroom with a sloped mattress. It felt strange to see these things through the window, but the place wasn't big enough not to notice. Nobody lurked in the rooms. No shadows shifted.

Stan wasn't home.

Christine's knees clacked together. She pressed her palms against the door and whispered, "I don't know what to do. I don't know what to do," over and over again. It all seemed so meaningless: her mother's affair with Stan, Stan leaving the boat lights off, and then her mother's death, Audrey's pregnancy, and now, Christine's stupid lust for Zach. None of it seemed to lead to anything else.

"Why did you love him, Mom?" she whispered, tilting her head back. She spoke to the sky, but it said nothing back. She'd heard from others who had lost their mothers that speaking to the heavens helped them; it gave them some kind of peace. She had never been able to find that kind of peace. She'd never really heard her mother answer back.

Overwhelmed with emotion, Christine banged her fist again on the outside screen door so hard that the thicker, main door creaked open. Of course, so far from anyone else, Stan hadn't locked his door. Christine's heart thudded in her chest so hard she thought it would burst through her ribcage. Did she have it in her to go inside, to wait for him to arrive? She imagined herself seated at his kitchen table, a glass of whiskey in front of her. She imagined what she might say and how startled he would be.

"You thought you would get away with it, didn't you? You thought you would never have to pay for what you did to us."

Christine's phone buzzed. She'd hardly imagined she would have service so far out there, and the sound of it shocked her. She glanced down to see Susan's name.

"Hey, Susan. What's up? How's Boston?" she asked. She placed a hand on her hip. She felt as though she'd been caught doing something she shouldn't have, as though Susan could fully see her and what she was up to.

"We're actually on the ferry on our way back," Susan said.

"Oh! What a surprise," Christine said. She struggled to brighten her voice. "Maybe we can order a pizza or something and you can tell us what happened. Sounds like you're getting closer and closer to Chuck."

"Yeah. Pizza sounds good," Susan said. Her words crackled. "Actually, I just want everyone to be back at the house as soon as possible. Scott and I have something to tell everyone."

"Oh, my God. Are you pregnant, too?" Christine asked, letting out a laugh knowing full well how much of a joke that was meant to be.

Susan was quiet for a long time. At first, Christine's heart seized. At forty-four, it wasn't completely outside the bounds of reason, right?

"Haha. No, I'm not," Susan finally said. "Just say you'll be there when we get back."

"Okay. I'll be there."

Christine blinked into Stan's house as she placed the phone back in her purse. Again, it felt as though the universe had shifted around her. This—whatever this was felt totally frivolous. She turned and fled and smashed her foot on the gas, no longer going the recommended five miles per hour. Whatever Susan was about to tell them, it wasn't good.

Christine could feel it in her bones.

CHAPTER 18

BACK AT THE HOUSE, AUDREY AND LOLA SAT AND SWUNG ON the porch swing, while Wes studied his glass of wine with somber eyes. The old radio near the door crackled songs from long-ago summers. When Christine walked out onto the porch, nobody's eyes looked toward her. Everyone simmered with their own internal thoughts and problems.

"Did she tell you anything about what it might be?" Christine finally tried.

Lola clicked her head left, then right, almost robotically. "Nope. But she sounded... bad."

"I know. She hasn't sounded like herself in a few weeks," Christine said.

Lola scrubbed her fingers over her eyes, rose, and poured herself and Christine both healthy glasses of wine. Audrey moaned and placed her hands over her stomach.

"Are you okay?" Christine asked.

"I thought I had avoided morning sickness, but it just kind of happens whenever it wants right now," Audrey murmured.

Christine placed her hand on Wes's shoulder and said, "Hey, Dad. How are you feeling?"

Wes gave her a sad smile and said, "I just want to find out what's wrong. The waiting is always the worst part."

"Maybe it really is about Chuck," Christine tried. "Susan's been hard at work trying to crack where that guy ran off to. I don't think we should jump to conclusions, though."

Scott's truck creaked into the driveway on the other side of the house. Everyone froze. Christine watched the inside of the house as first Scott entered, then Susan. Both carried pizza boxes, enough to feed a huge family. It was a common thing in any family to overcompensate when things went wrong.

The screen door slammed behind them as they joined the others on the porch. Susan and Scott placed the pizza boxes on the picnic table, as Susan tried on a fake smile.

"Hey, everyone," she said, giving them her best smile.

"Hey, Aunt Susie," Audrey said.

"You're looking a little green," Susan said, her brow furrowed.

"It's just the baby," Audrey said. "It's clearing up, though. I bet I'll be hungrier than ever in a few minutes. That seems to be the rhythm."

Susan tried on a laugh. Lola cleared her throat and shifted in the porch swing, gesturing for Susan to sit. Susan shook her head and said, "Actually, I would prefer to stand, if that's okay."

Christine glanced again at Scott. To her surprise, he looked absolutely downtrodden, like a dog left out in the rain. Christine's heart sank. Something was really wrong.

"We actually went up to Boston to receive the results of a test I took a few weeks ago," Susan said suddenly.

"What kind of test?" Lola demanded.

Scott placed his hand on Susan's shoulder. Christine cupped both elbows with her hands as she started to shake. She hadn't been in this kind of conversation since Wes had told them about their mother. It felt like having your insides mashed up with a meat grinder.

"I thought maybe I could get away without saying anything," Susan continued. "Around the time of the divorce, I had minor surgery for stage II breast cancer. They thought they got everything. I came back to the Vineyard with the idea that I could begin a new life here, without the drama and the medical ailments of my past. But it seems like I haven't escaped it fully. The cancer has moved to stage III, and they want me to start chemotherapy as soon as possible."

Lola's jaw dropped. Silence filled the porch as Susan scrunched her eyes together. To Christine, receiving the news felt like getting hit by a car. The impact sent wave after wave of pain across her stomach, her heart and her head.

"Wait. I don't understand," Lola said. Her voice was edged with anger. "You hid this from us all this time? During this time, when we promised, there would be no more secrets between us? After learning about how Mom really died?"

Wes let out a horrible sob, the kind only an older man could: one that filled everyone else with endless sorrow because there was nothing to be done.

Christine interjected, "Lola, stop! You can't blame her for that.

We only just all came back to the Vineyard. I'm sure it's been a difficult thing to wage..."

Even as she heard herself speak, Christine hardly understood anything about this at all. Now, everything clicked into place like puzzle pieces in their father's puzzle. The medical marijuana. Of course. Susan Sheridan wouldn't have been the type of woman to start smoking weed in her forties.

Christine should have known something was really off. It had been right there in front of her. Maybe she'd been too selfish about her own career, the loss of Chez Frank and her strange, newfound love for Zach to take any notice.

Wes pressed both his hands to his cheeks. His shoulders shook. Immediately, Christine rushed toward him and wrapped her arms around him. As the world shifted around him, as his memory crumbled, more and more horrors made themselves known. He shook and cried as Christine held him and felt her own tears roll down her cheeks.

Audrey gripped her stomach with one hand, her mouth with her other, and fumbled off the porch. Christine thought she might throw up, too, watching her. Lola stood slowly, making the porch swing creak back and forth behind her. Her blue eyes looked enormous and volatile.

"I'm sorry, Lola. I really thought I was in the clear. I thought I was going to be okay," Susan murmured.

Susan's voice broke and wavered. This was their big sister, the woman they'd both looked up to throughout their entire lives, even from afar—breaking down in front of them. Christine, who had never been the one anyone could ever lean on, not in any context, kept her hand on her father's back and wrapped Susan in a huge bear hug with the other.

"It's going to be okay, Susan," she said. "We've got this." To her ears, she sounded much more like Anna than herself. "Seriously. You're the strongest woman that any of us know. This is just another hiccup. You fought through all the other battles of the past few years. Why not this, too?"

Through tears, Susan started to laugh. The sound was a huge surprise, and Christine ducked back to look at her. Had she lost her mind? But instead, through a sad smile, Susan said, "I've never heard you like this before, Christine."

Christine rolled her eyes. Devastation hollowed itself in every area of her body as she held her sister closer than ever. "I don't know why we have to take this opportunity to pinpoint just how dead inside I've been all my life."

Lola laughed now, too. "Look at you! Christine! Susan!" She rushed to them and wrapped her arms around them, too. "Susie, I'm so sorry I was angry. I'm not, really. I'm just shocked and scared. But Susie, we're going to get you through this, the way we've gotten through everything else." Her eyes peered across their hug, latching on Wes. "Don't you think so, Dad?"

Slowly, Wes removed his hands from his eyes and turned toward them. He looked strange, his skin grey, but he managed a smile. "You girls are stronger than Anna and I ever were. You've seen things, created lives for yourselves, and still, you have each other, here." He glanced toward Scott, who looked on the verge of losing it. "Me and Scott are the luckiest men alive to be in your presence right now."

Scott walked over to Wes and wrapped an arm around his

shoulder. "You got that right." he said as he wiped a tear from the corner of his eye.

Exhausted, the Sheridan sisters, Scott, and Wes sat down several minutes later to nibble at the once-forgotten pizza. Throughout the meal, Susan tried her best to explain some of the other things her doctor had told her. The survival rate was okay: not the kind of number to write home about, exactly, but decent enough. She also explained that chemotherapy could happen right there on the island, which meant that the sisters could help her to and from. Scott would also always be around for any support.

"Imagine me trying to put this burden on my children," Susan said. "Jake's all bogged down with the twins, and Amanda is in the middle of her internship and also planning her wedding."

"They would have done anything for you, and you know it," Lola said. "Don't be silly. But we're happy to help out here. Heck. I'd say the only real issue we have right now is the lack of space in this place."

Scott cleared his throat and smeared his napkin across his lips. "I'm going to start on a project right away." He pointed toward the wall alongside the kitchen and dining area and said, "That whole space over there. I want to extend it out and make two more bedrooms. It shouldn't take too long if I hire a few contractors to help me. It's the kind of thing I used to do all the time, years ago when I did Frampton Freight alongside a bit of building work."

"That's right. I hired you to fix up part of the Inn years ago when that hurricane hit part of the bistro," Wes affirmed.

Again, Christine and Susan locked eyes, shocked at Wes's memory.

"You did a swell job, Scott," Wes said. "I wouldn't want anyone else to touch my beautiful house but you."

"There's no telling how long all of us will be here, but I want to make sure it's cozy enough for all of you," Scott said. "Just three bedrooms upstairs isn't cutting it."

"You're telling me," Audrey said as she swung out from the main house. Her eyes were tinged with red, and her cheeks looked hollowed out. She stepped toward Susan and dropped down to hug her. She seemed unable to muster any words.

"Come on, Audrey. It hasn't been so bad sharing a room with your old Mom, has it?" Lola laughed.

Audrey rolled her eyes. "We went from having no family to us all living on top of each other. What a sitcom." She grabbed a slice of pizza and splayed it across an old plate, one Christine recognized from her girlhood. She then sat next to Christine and placed her head against her shoulder. "I'm glad we have each other. Let's keep it that way."

The words nearly made Christine's heart explode.

That night, Susan decided to head to Scott's to sleep, while Christine, Lola, and Audrey sat out on the porch and stared at the water, all dumbfounded. A bit awkwardly, Lola tried to talk to Audrey about elements of the current story she wrote about another Boston socialite; Audrey had her own opinions about how she should tackle the interview, which Lola seemed to listen to with curiosity and respect, despite her years in the business.

Christine's phone buzzed to reveal a text from Zach.

ZACH WALTERS: Hey. Sorry about earlier today. Do you mind if I call you to explain it?

With all the commotion of the previous hours, the Zach drama felt like it had happened a million years ago. Remy, the girl from his apparently not-so-long-ago past, had been lurking around his house on his day off and had been crying when Christine had arrived. Remy, who seemed, in nearly every way, to be better than Christine for the likes of Zach.

After all, Christine had spent the past twenty-odd years hating Zach Walters. She could go back to a mild level of distaste, especially since she planned to remain on the island to care for her sister.

CHRISTINE: Naw, it's cool. I shouldn't have stopped by like that. I have a little bit of a family crisis going on at the moment and need to take the next few days off. I hope that's okay.

Lola arched her brow as Christine set her phone back down. "What was that about?"

"What do you mean?"

"You looked like you just had to make some kind of gut-wrenching decision," Lola said with a laugh.

"What? No," Christine said, furrowing her brow.

"I'm your sister. I can sense it," Lola said.

"Naw. Just asking for a few days off from work, so I can focus on family," Christine said. "I don't think I can manage to fold up another croissant for another hungry tourist right now."

"Fair enough," Lola said.

ZACH WALTERS: Ok. I hope everything's okay? Please, let me know if there's anything I can do.

This was Vineyard neighborly kindness and nothing more. Christine knew this. She pressed the "END" button and let her phone fade to black. Zach Walters and the rest of the world could wait.

CHAPTER 19

SUSAN'S FIRST CHEMOTHERAPY SESSION BEGAN AT 2:30 IN THE afternoon on the following Monday. On the drive to the hospital, Lola drove, Susan sat in the passenger seat, and Christine sat in the back, her eyes scanning the thick line of trees and spotting shadows from birds that flew high in the sky. When they reached the hospital, Lola turned down the radio and glanced at Susan.

"Are you ready?"

"As ready as I'll ever be," Susan announced.

As they entered the cancer wing, Susan texted something to Amanda and Jake, who she'd told about the cancer three days before. Apparently, Amanda had nearly quit her internship on the spot in order to come care for her mom, but Susan had insisted she stay.

"She's still threatening to come here," Susan said, stalling in the lobby of the cancer wing. "But what would she do here? She would just sit around and be worried about me. I couldn't handle that."

"She just loves you," Lola said, sliding her hand up and down Susan's arm. "And she's so much like you. She just wants to make sure everyone is okay all the time."

At the front desk, Susan collected a clipboard and filled out her information, while Lola and Christine made light chitchat with the receptionist, whom they had gone to school with. When they finally retreated, Lola muttered in Christine's ear, "I never liked her. Of course, she works here. She likes to see everyone on their worst day."

"What did you say? I couldn't hear it," Susan said with a smile.

"Nothing," Lola said.

"She's just being difficult as always," Christine said, trying the joke.

"Isn't that your thing, Christine?" Lola asked.

The receptionist placed her finger over her lips and shushed them, which cast all three of them into reckless giggles. Christine had always marveled about this: during some of the bigger days of her life, funerals and weddings and anything else, when emotions were heightened, the laughter came easier, regardless of how sad it all was.

When Susan was called in for chemo, Lola and Christine stepped out onto the back porch of the hospital, which looked out over some of the docks that held tourist yachts, sailboats, and even a few fishing boats from the locals. Lola grabbed her elbows, anxious, and said, "I just don't know what to do with myself while she's in there."

"It's surreal, isn't it?" Christine murmured. She dropped her purse to the ground and stretched out her arms, touching her toes. As she lingered down there, Lola let out a strange, shocking noise.

"What's wrong?" Christine asked, lifting her head ever so slightly.

"I see him."

"Who?" Christine demanded.

"Stan. Ellis," Lola said. "He's always everywhere, isn't he? He's our stupid rat. We can't get rid of him."

Christine hadn't bothered to inform her sisters that she had actually gone to Stan's house.

She stood and followed Lola's gaze out across the docks, toward a gorgeous sailboat. Stan Ellis stood with his hands on his hips, speaking to a man who seemed to be approximately six-foot-five, a half-foot taller than Stan, with broad shoulders and dark, curly hair, the kind that was taken directly from a romance novel.

"And who is he talking to?" Christine asked, furrowing her brow.

"I guess he's the owner of that boat," Lola said. "I just saw him hop off and tie it up."

"Maybe they're just fishing friends?" Christine offered.

"Who knows," Lola said. "The Round-the-Island Race is coming up. Maybe he's racing in it? That's certainly the kind of boat that he would need to win."

"Hmm." Christine kept her eyes toward Stan, hardly hearing what Lola said about the handsome stranger.

"I'm actually supposed to write about the race for an online magazine," Lola said suddenly.

"Oh?"

"And supposed to interview a sailor in the race," Lola continued.

Christine arched her brow. She hardly had energy to stand

there on the porch, waiting for Susan's chemotherapy to end, let alone consider whatever story possibility Lola had with the guy who now spoke to Stan Ellis. Still, the second Stan Ellis stepped away from the stranger Lola cut across the porch and headed toward the staircase that led to the docks. Christine barreled after her, not wanting to be left alone.

"What are you doing?" Christine hissed.

Lola pressed her shoulders back, a portrait of arrogance. "I just want to talk to him. That's all."

As they marched down the dock, it creaked beneath them, casting them to the left and right with the slam and ease of the waves. The stranger continued to organize the interior of his sailboat and pile things into a large black backpack. When they got close enough, they could hear him whistling an old sea shanty.

When they reached him, he turned around slowly, so that his dark eyes locked onto Lola's with cinematic power. Lola, who wasn't afraid of anything, stood her ground.

"Hello, ladies," the man bellowed out in a cheerful greeting. "What can I do for you?"

"Hey there," Lola said. She shot her hand out to shake his. "My name is Lola Sheridan, and I'm a journalist covering the Round-the-Island race. I was wondering. Are you racing in it this year?"

The man spread his arms out in either direction and said, "What was your first clue?"

Lola laughed good-naturedly. "Fantastic. I would love to feature you in my next piece about the race."

"An interview, huh? What makes you think you deserve my flair for language in your piece?" he asked.

Lola grabbed her business card and placed it in his

outstretched hand. "I would really appreciate it," she said. "By the way. I saw you chatting with Stan Ellis before. How do you know him?"

The man gave her a curious look. "Stan Ellis is my ex-step-father," he said. He and my mom split up when I was twelve or thirteen before he came to the island."

Christine's jaw dropped. Her eyes flashed toward Lola, trying to catch any sign of what she thought of any of this. But Lola was accustomed to this kind of journalistic endeavor.

"Interesting," Lola said. "What did you say your name was again?"

"I didn't," the man said. "I'm Tommy. Tom Gasbarro. My dad was, or, is, Italian, but he left Mom and I when I was really little before she met Stan. It didn't work out, but Stan was the only father figure I ever really had. I try to race in the Round-the-Island race every year, just to meet up with him and reconnect. He's something of a loner out here, I think, although it's difficult to get the full picture."

Christine's heart panged. Lola's smile was still very difficult to read. "It's really good to meet you. I hope we can meet for that chat before the race. My editors would be very pleased, to say the least, especially given your experience with the race."

"Sounds good, Lola. Thanks a lot," Tommy said, flashing them both one last smile before they turned to walk away.

Christine and Lola returned to the cancer wing a few minutes later. Christine's heart beat wildly in her throat. They collapsed in the plastic chairs, again a little too loudly for the receptionist's liking, and turned their eyes to one another.

"Are you kidding me? Stan Ellis's ex-step-son," Lola breathed.

"This whole thing is getting weirder and weirder," Christine affirmed.

"Do you think he knows about Mom?"

"I have no idea," Christine said. "He didn't jump or anything when he heard your last name." She paused and tilted her head. "He's really handsome, isn't he?"

Lola flipped her hand around exasperated. "Sure. I mean, he's got that whole sailor vibe, doesn't he? It probably works on all the girls."

"It certainly worked on you," Christine said, giving her little sister a knowingly nudge.

Lola rolled her eyes. "Don't be stupid. I'm just trying to get the story." Her eyes flashed. "Besides. Two can play this game. Why haven't you gone back to the bistro or even said Zach's name in the past few days?"

Christine gave Lola an eagle-eyed look. Lola chuckled. "That's what I thought."

The door out into the lobby opened to reveal Susan. She walked slowly, her eyes glistening, but her face stoic. Christine and Lola burst up from their plastic chairs and hustled to Susan.

"How did it go?" Lola demanded.

"Oh, fine," Susan said. Her voice was strangely far away. "I just want to go home."

Back in the car, Susan placed the top of her forehead against the window as Lola snaked the car back toward the main house. Lola messed with the radio station until it played a song that had come out during Christine's senior year of high school, "Lovefool," by The Cardigans. Gently, under her breath, Susan began to sing along.

"Love me, love me, pretend that you love me," she sang.

"So, I cry, and I beg for you to..." Lola sang.

"Love me! Love me!" Christine joined in. "Say that you'll love me!"

Large tears rolled down their cheeks by the time they reached the house. The song faded out and left them with the wild radio DJ bantering through the speakers.

"I remember when that song came out. Jake was just a baby. I was pretending to be the kind of new mom who knew how to do everything," Susan said. "I tried to make all my own baby food."

"Christine and I were probably in this very driveway listening to it," Lola offered.

"And singing at the tops of our lungs," Christine said.

"Some things never change, I guess," Susan said. "Other things change a lot."

That was the theme of the year, Christine thought.

Scott opened the screen door facing the driveway. His face was grey and apprehensive. He reached the car seconds later and brought open Susan's door. "Hey, baby. Hey." He helped her out and wrapped his arm around her shoulders, tucking her against him.

"Hey," she said. Her smile was more beautiful than ever. "Don't worry. I'm not going to collapse on you. The doctor just said I might vomit all over you in a few hours—nothing to worry about."

"Did someone say vomit?" This came from Audrey, who appeared in the doorway of the main house and opened the screen door wide for them all to enter. "Because I know all about that."

"I'm sure you do," Susan offered. She gave her a soft, knowing smile.

That evening, Wes, Scott, Susan, Audrey, Lola, and Christine sat out on the porch. It was a surprisingly chilly night, despite the lateness in July, and they wore sweatshirts and drank hot tea and watched the waves roll in. The conversation was either light or nonexistent, as though each of them had to live in their own sacred spaces, consider their own thoughts, and find meaning in them. Still, the company was necessary.

Since there was still so little space at the house, Scott and Susan left soon afterward to go sleep at his place. Christine and Lola glared at each other, daring the other to protest. When they left, they both blurted, "She should stay here! We need to take care of her!"

At this, Wes just shook his head. "Scott has her back. He always has."

There was so much truth to his words that they couldn't protest.

About a half-hour later, both Wes and Audrey escaped upstairs, leaving Christine and Lola out on the porch swing, rocking back and forth. Lola scrubbed her hands over her eyes.

"What a day," she marveled.

"One for the books," Christine returned. After a pause, she said, "I was amazed that you just walked up to that sailor guy like that. You had so much confidence. More than I've ever had."

"Are you kidding? You've traveled all over the world. You have so many experiences…"

Christine shrugged. "I still don't think I would have done something like that."

Lola pondered this for a long time. "I guess maybe it's been the magic of this summer. Or maybe the curse of it, I don't know. I know better than to waste any time, though. I wanted to know who that guy was, so I went over and figured it out myself. I hope he calls me for the interview."

Christine had a hunch that Lola wanted him to call for many other reasons, as well.

Still, her words rang through Christine's head that night as she tossed and turned in bed. At forty-one years old, she was still strong, both emotionally and physically; she had years of potential happiness ahead of her. All around her were reasons for her to push herself to build the life she'd always wanted.

Lola was right. She couldn't waste anything anymore.

Least of all... time.

CHAPTER 20

THE NEXT DAY, SCOTT TEXTED CHRISTINE AND LOLA TO SAY that Susan was more wiped out than ever. When Christine went down to the kitchen around seven, she found Audrey curled up in a ball by the floor near the couch, her head on a pillow. Christine grabbed a glass and filled it with water, to place near Audrey, just in case.

"You okay, pumpkin?" she asked her.

"Oh, yes. Just a minor infestation in the uterus region," Audrey tried to joke.

"You're the funniest of all of us, even when you're sick," Christine said, placing her hand across Audrey's forehead.

Audrey grimaced and said, "You would have been a really good mom, Christine. Just in case you needed to know that."

Christine was surprised that this didn't shock her or hurt her or make her feel small. Instead, she gave the girl a delicate smile and told her to call her if she needed anything. "I'll be here until just after lunch. Then, I have a job to do."

Audrey rushed up and heaved toward the bathroom again, leaving the pillow and water glass behind. Felix snuck around the side of the couch, his eyes buggy as he meowed.

"Where have you been?" Christine asked him, stroking his glossy back.

From the bathroom, Audrey called, "He sleeps with me a lot. Sorry."

Christine laughed. "He probably knows you need the extra comfort. He's good like that."

In response, Felix let out another meow.

Christine joined Wes out on the picnic table and helped him stitch a few puzzle pieces into place. He nibbled on a croissant, which Scott had brought over the previous day from the Oak Bluffs bakery. "They're just not the same," Wes said of the croissants. "Not as buttery. Not as flaky. How do you do it, Christine?"

"I sold a French pastry chef my soul," Christine said, giving her dad a wink.

Wes chuckled. "Normally, I wouldn't condone something like that, but in this case..."

Buzzing with excitement for the next few hours, Christine did anything she could to keep her mind focused. When Audrey felt a bit better, they did some yoga stretches near the water, their chests arched toward the sky. She let Audrey paint her fingernails and tell her about some of her favorite boys from school, leaving out any news about the guy who'd gotten her pregnant in Chicago. It seemed like nothing had changed in that department, anyway.

"I loved college so much," Audrey said with a heavy sigh. "I don't know how I'm going to say goodbye to it. College parties... late-nights at the dorms with my new best friends..." She buzzed her lips as she smeared another dark purple line across Christine's left ring finger. "Oh, but it's not good to dwell on it. It'll poison me."

Just after three in the afternoon, Christine donned a white sundress, a pair of sandals, and an old gold necklace that had belonged to her mother's. She pulled her shoulders back, checked her makeup, added another gloss of lipstick, and then walked toward the bistro. Her heart pumped like a bass drum, and she felt dizzy with every step.

But she couldn't waste any more time.

When she appeared in the bistro kitchen, she found Zach in conversation with Ronnie and another cook. Immediately, Ronnie's face broke into an exuberant smile.

"Christine!" Ronnie rushed toward her and wrapped her in a huge hug. "I was so worried you wouldn't come back."

Zach's smile was difficult to read. She hadn't contacted him at all over the past week. The air between them was strained.

"Hey there," he said.

"Hey. Lunch rush over?" Christine said.

"Yeah. Decent rush," Zach said. "I was about to head out."

"Right. I figured," Christine said.

The cook and Ronnie exchanged glances. Christine opened her lips and closed them again, suddenly worried she'd done the wrong thing all over again.

Suddenly, another of the busboys burst through the swinging kitchen door and cried, "We have a situation!"

"What's up?" Zach asked. He seemed grateful to deal with anything else.

"Shamala is here," the busboy said. He was breathless. "She just filmed a music video on a yacht, and they want to eat."

"Shamala?" Zach and Christine asked simultaneously.

Ronnie rolled his eyes. "Christine, come on. I told you about her. She's a huge YouTube star, and she just signed her first major label. This. Is. Huge. She has maybe two or three million Instagram fans, so anything she posts..."

Zach's eyes grew huge. "How many people are in the cast and crew?"

The other busboy poked his head out the door again. When he returned, he coughed and said, "They filled up the whole bistro again."

"Shoot. Okay. Nobody leaves!" Zach cried. He leaped toward the door and entered the dining area again, surging toward the girl who seemed to be Shamala—an early twenties-something with gorgeous, inky hair, wearing a crop-top and typing out something she seemed bored with on her phone.

Christine had been in situations like this countless times. Immediately, she scrubbed up her hands, grabbed an apron, and jumped in to help. The orders flew in fast and loose, and she found herself pouring drinks, flipping burgers, checking on fish, and drizzling lemon over everything. The kitchen staff and wait staff swirled into a kind of chaotic, but workable rhythm, until all members of the cast and crew had a plate in front of them, ready to eat.

Zach crashed hard against the side of the kitchen wall about an hour later. Sweat billowed down his back. Ronnie stomped into the kitchen, wrinkled up his apron, and cried, "I've never been more exhausted in my life! But I think I might be in her Instagram story!"

Christine and Zach burst into laughter. Suddenly, it felt as though all the drama and awkwardness between them floated away. They'd been united to craft the perfect late-lunch rush for some celebrity, and they'd done it without a hitch.

As the kitchen staff cleaned up, Zach approached Christine and leaned close to her ear. "Could I interest you in a drink at my place? No pressure, if not."

Before she gave a thought to what she did, Christine found herself in the front seat of Zach's pick-up, watching Oak Bluffs trade itself out for Edgartown. She half-expected Zach to say something about how she had found his place without asking him the week before, but luckily, he seemed not to care. When they parked in the front, he said, "I have craft beer and wine and something a little bit stronger. What are you game for?"

"I'll drink anything right now. I'm just as tired as Ronnie. Maybe even more."

"And the poor kid has to wash down the pain with ice cream," Zach said with a laugh.

Zach's porch had a gorgeous view of the water. His dock was located next to a healthy line of large thick trees, and he had let a lilac bush take over much of that area of the yard so that it looked like a firework of purple color. Christine sat, watching as he poured her a glass of chardonnay.

"Not in a styrofoam cup this time," she said. "Impressive."

"Ha. Doesn't that seem like months ago? Time on this island in the summer is bizarre," Zach said.

They clinked glasses and sat in separate rocking chairs, gazing out toward the Nantucket Sound. Secrets, questions, their past, swirled around them ominously.

Finally, Christine said, "My sisters could never remember why I hated you so much."

Zach cut her that attractive smile again. Christine felt strangely comfortable like she could tell him anything.

"It's so stupid, but, I really liked you, you know," she said. "And you dumped me right before we went head-to-head in that stupid cooking competition."

"What! I didn't dump you," Zach protested. His eyes nearly bugged out of his head. "No. Someone told me they saw you making out with that trombone player. Peter."

Christine furrowed her brow and had to try to think back. Had she done that?

"No way. I don't remember anyone named Peter," she said.

"You looked pretty cozy with him the week after that," Zach affirmed with a shrug. "I was so mad at you during our cooking competition."

"I was so mad at you! We were supposed to go swimming the night before, but you dropped me off early and wouldn't tell me what was wrong," Christine said.

Zach's eyes glittered with humor. "This is ridiculous. Both of us thought the other one wronged each other."

"For all these years," Christine finished.

"It's kind of a miracle that we're here together now," Zach said.

Christine nodded as her heart jumped. After a pause, she said, "I'm sorry I stormed over here like that. I guess I thought things were a bit different, or something, and I..."

"Christine, it isn't your fault. Actually, that has nothing to do with you. I was upset that you saw her and I like that because I knew what you would think. But the truth is..."

He took a deep breath. Christine's mind went a million directions without finding any kind of conclusion.

Finally, he said, "Remy and I met in Boston when we were both in culinary school. I was in my late twenties and she was a tiny bit younger. We hit it off, but it wasn't anything really serious until suddenly, she got pregnant."

Christine felt as though someone had wrapped a hand around her throat and squeezed hard.

Zach took a sip of his chardonnay and studied the water. "What do you do in that situation? I don't know. It's different for everyone. But Remy and I decided to try to make it work. She had our baby, a daughter, and we were happy, really happy, for about a year after her birth.

"Quinn was about fourteen months old when it happened. I was driving Remy and Quinn and me out to dinner to celebrate. Remy had just been offered a fantastic chef position at a new French spot in downtown Boston. Our lives felt like they were on the up-and-up, with no down in sight. But the truck came out of nowhere. It ran a red light and T-boned us and smashed us into a light post in the middle of an intersection. I remember the last thing I saw before lights out: Remy laughing at something Quinn had done."

Christine hadn't been able to breathe in what felt like years. She clenched her eyes tight, then forced herself to open them and let out the breath she had been holding. She owed it to Zach to hear the whole thing.

"I was in a coma for about a week," Zach continued. "I can't describe what it felt like to wake up from that. The first thing I realized was that time had passed, that I didn't know where my girlfriend or my daughter, Quinn, was. That's when they told me that Quinn hadn't made it. Remy had moved in with her mother already. While I'd been unconscious, they'd gone through all of Quinn's things and taken them out of the house. That made me so angry, Christine. Those were my memories, too. It was like I had woken up in a world I didn't know, one without my baby girl. The one person I had endless love for."

A single sob escaped his throat. Christine reached over and gripped his hand, surprising herself.

"I haven't talked to that many people on the island about it," he said. "My friends know, of course. My mom, who's still around. But nobody really knows what to say. Plus, I came back to get away from the pain the outside world caused, you know? All my life, I had wanted to get off this island. And then, I realized, it's the only home I really know or want."

Remy. A woman who had gone through so much more pain than Christine could fully comprehend. She clenched her eyes tight and slipped her fingers further into Zach's grip.

"We finally started talking a few years ago," Zach admitted. "And we check in with one another. Remy has another kid back in Boston, but she doesn't like to talk to me about him. We spent most of the day together talking about her, about our memories of her. It's our only way to keep her alive in our hearts."

As he spoke, storm clouds brewed over the Nantucket Sound. Rain splattered across the little steps that led from the water, up toward his little stone cottage. The sound was soothing, a reminder that all terrible things eventually washed away.

Slowly, Zach and Christine found ways to talk about other things. He shared a few memories of his daughter, while she explained the severity of losing her ovary and learning she could never fully fulfill her dreams of having a baby of her own. He listened, allowing her to hold her own grief, yet supporting her in it as much as he could.

As night crept over them, Zach and Christine piled onto the mattress on the first floor of the house and held one another close, fully clothed, their hearts beating as one. Christine felt closer to this man than she had any other person she had met in years. As he drifted off to sleep, she caught herself trying to memorize the lines on his face, the soft smile that remained even in slumber. She prayed that if they couldn't find a way to any kind of a happy ending that she would remember this moment for the rest of her life.

It felt like beautiful freedom from a past she no longer had to fully understand.

CHAPTER 21

A FEW DAYS LATER, CHRISTINE FINISHED HER SHIFT AT THE bistro around ten in the morning. She met Zach in the office. He studied some paperwork, his finger tracing the lines as he mumbled to himself. Frankly, it was adorable.

Still, even though they'd slept next to one another, Christine and Zach hadn't kissed or touched one another at all since that night. It hadn't been awkward between them, per se, only pregnant with expectation. What would happen next? It felt like a romantic nail biter.

"Hey there," Christine said, catching him off-guard.

Zach turned up his face, wide-eyed, and said, "Oh, Christine. Hey. Sorry, I always get so lost in the numbers." As his grin widened, Christine caught his eyes running down her face, down to her legs.

She loved the idea that he liked the way she looked, even over twenty years after they'd first tried their hand at romance. Even at age forty-one.

"Can I help you with anything before I go?" Christine asked.

Zach's eyes seemed playful. "Anything at all?"

"Hmm. Seems like a trick question," Christine said, her hand on her hips.

Zach clicked his tongue. He rose himself to his full height, then reached over and grabbed a strand of her dark hair to curl it over her ear. Still, he didn't kiss her. Christine thought her head might explode.

"Here's what I want you to do," Zach said. "Susan mentioned the other day that her daughter, Amanda, is coming today. I set aside a whole basket of your scrumptious croissants in a basket over near the walk-in. Make sure you take it with you."

"I almost forgot!" Christine said. Her eyes refused to do anything else but live in the enormity of his. "Thank you, Zach. I appreciate it."

Christine buzzed with excitement as she approached the family house. Over the past several days, Scott and a few contractors had dug up the ground next to it and put a foundation in. Already, wooden boards outlined what would be two more bedrooms. Christine, Susan, and Lola couldn't wait to dig in and start the decoration process, something Scott had already said wasn't his forte. "You should see the interior design at his place," Susan had joked.

Susan had had another chemo session the day before, which meant that today, the house was a bit more subdued, shadowed. Susan sat on the sofa, beneath a heavy winter blanket, with Amanda beside her, her head on her mother's shoulder. Audrey sat in the chair across from them, sipping tea, while Lola hovered in the kitchen, seemingly unsure of what to offer whom.

"Hi everyone," Christine said. She placed the basket of croissants on the counter and beamed at Amanda. "It's so good to see you again. Your mom is so thrilled you're here."

Amanda blinked back tears. She stood and hugged Christine and then returned to her mother's side.

"She's taking good care of me," Susan said. "All of you are. I finally had to shoo Scott away. Someone has to take care of the Inn while I'm like this. All the work I've done over the past summer can't fly out the window."

"Did it hit you a bit harder this time?" Christine asked.

"A little," Susan said. "I'm tired, but the nausea faded. Actually, I've invited Charlotte and Rachel over for a conversation with Amanda. We're so stuck on wedding planning, and I don't want to get further behind."

Charlotte worked in event planning on the island, frequently with her daughter Rachel. After Charlotte's husband's death, Charlotte and Rachel had thrown themselves as much as possible into the business, even supporting a celebrity's wedding earlier in the summer.

"So you're thinking about having the wedding on the Vineyard, then?" Christine asked.

"Absolutely," Amanda returned. "I told my fiancé about the vibe of the place, and he's already fallen in love. I wish he could come out this summer to see everything, but he's been so slammed with work."

"It's not like you want him to help you with the wedding planning, anyway," Susan said with a smile.

"I'm no more a control freak than you are," Amanda said, giggling.

"Oh, so you're pretty bad, then," Lola said.

"Ha, yes. I guess so," Amanda admitted. "My friends always said if you know Susan or Amanda, you know both of them."

Christine's heart burned with envy, but she made sure she didn't show it. Instead, she passed out the croissants, made another batch of coffee, and greeted both Charlotte and Rachel with big hugs when they arrived.

The air sizzled with excitement as the women of the Sheridan clan dove into wedding conversation. Charlotte listed some of the most popular venues on the island, including the beautiful Union Chapel, the White Cliffs Country Club, or the Sunrise Cove Inn itself, of course.

Amanda hovered in the middle of all of them at the picnic table, with about five different bride and wedding magazines spread out in front of her. She furrowed her brow as she listened to Charlotte's advice, and then turned her eyes to her mother, checking in with her opinion. Across the table from them, Audrey sat with her fists under her chin, frowning at the wedding magazines.

How strange it was, Christine thought. Amanda's whole life was headed for glory and excitement. She would be a criminal lawyer like her mother; she would marry the man of her dreams. Probably very soon, she would have first one bouncing baby, and then another until her life very much resembled her mother's from a few years before. By contrast, Audrey was pregnant with a man's baby she wanted nothing to do with, and her life was now put on hold.

"What do you think of this low-cut style, Audrey?" Amanda said. Her eyes snapped up toward her cousin.

Audrey blinked. "Why would you ask me?" she said with a laugh.

"I stalked your Instagram. Your fashion sense is insane," Amanda said sheepishly. "I totally respect your opinion."

"Isn't that nice," Lola said. "We're a family of fashionistas."

Audrey looked strained. She glanced down at her ratty t-shirt, which, Christine had noticed, she had worn the past two days. "I guess you've caught me at a bad time for something like that," she offered, trying to keep her smile plastered across her face.

"Oh. It's summer. Who cares," Amanda said. "But this cut. Do you think it was more in fashion five years ago? Or would it be okay?"

Christine peered over Amanda's shoulder to spot the lacey long-sleeved number, which surged down between the bride's breasts. Audrey shook her head and scrunched her nose. "I think it's just a little too... Mariah Carey."

Amanda burst into laughter. "Chris isn't exactly Nick Cannon."

"Let's keep looking," Susan said. Her hand padded the top of her hair mindlessly as her eyes scanned the page. Soon, all her hair would be gone.

Suddenly, Audrey bucked up from the picnic table. Lola arched her brow as Audrey said, "I'll be right back, Mom. Don't worry about it."

"I didn't say anything!" Lola cried.

"I know. But you wanted to," Audrey returned.

Christine watched as Audrey snuck down the porch steps,

toward the water. Almost immediately, the women sprung into a conversation about wedding colors, what music to play while Amanda walked down the aisle, and how much Amanda actually wanted her father, Richard, involved. Sure, she loved him; he was her dad. But he'd also cheated on her mother and destroyed her family, so she wasn't always keen on the idea of him walking her down the aisle.

"I'd rather have you walk me, Mom," Amanda said, looking at her mother with tears in her eyes.

As the chatter continued, Christine stood and followed Audrey down toward the water. The beautiful girl sat at the edge of the dock; her bare feet dipped into the water and her eyes toward the horizon. When Christine reached her, she said, "Hey. What's on your mind?"

Audrey spun her head around quickly but didn't smile. "Oh. Hey."

"Can I sit with you for a minute?" Christine asked. "All the mother-daughter talk is getting to be a lot."

Audrey nodded. "I'm sure it must get annoying. And none of us realize we're doing it. Making you feel left out."

The waves rushed faster over the tiny rocks that lined the shore. Christine cleared her throat and said, "It's really okay."

"No. It's not," Audrey continued. She stared at the water, her eyes reflecting the light. "I hate it up there right now. Amanda is so excited about this next phase of her life. She's done everything the right way, and Susan just adores her. Meanwhile, I can see my mom's eyes on me, adding me up in her head. I'm such a disappointment."

Christine's tongue felt glued to the bottom of her mouth. She knew, in situations such as this, it was never possible to say the right thing.

"I'm going to have this baby, and then what?" Audrey continued. "Move back to college? Get a crummy apartment and a crummy job and take as many classes as I can? I'm picturing the two of us in some dingy, dark place like the place I first remember Mom and I living in and I feel overwhelmed with it all. It's a huge weight. I know it's my fault that I have to live with what I've done. But I just can't..."

Suddenly, her words flung themselves out of Christine's mouth so fast that she wasn't able to catch them.

"I will raise your baby."

Audrey's jaw dropped. She looked at Christine as though she'd never seen her before in her life. "What do you mean?"

Christine felt a tiny bit flustered, but, at the same time, clearer than she had in months.

"You're only about six weeks into your pregnancy, so it's a long way down the road," Christine continued. "But you would only have to miss two semesters. Then, you could go back to school, back to your scholarship, back to your friends. You could probably even make up some of your classes over next summer or online so that you could graduate on time. I'm not sure how it all works."

Audrey's look was pinched, intense. For a moment, Christine thought she'd marched far, far over the line of propriety.

"I know it will be a difficult thing, especially because you probably already love this baby more than you understand," Christine continued. "But you can be involved in the baby's life in every possible way. I'll just be Aunt Christine. And you can be with your baby again whenever you're ready."

Audrey's nostrils flared as she considered her aunt's words. Again, Christine thought she would rip her into shreds at such a ridiculous idea.

But seconds later, Audrey murmured, "It might work and would help in almost every single way."

Christine's heart leaped into her throat. Her voice cracked as she whispered, "Really? Are you sure?"

Audrey nodded slowly, her eyebrows still low. "I can't think of a single reason why this shouldn't or couldn't work."

Christine flung her arms around Audrey and held her close. Before she realized it, a sob rippled through her body as the two of them hugged on the dock.

A baby.

This was the baby she had always wanted.

CHAPTER 22

THE EDGARTOWN ROUND-THE-ISLAND RACE WAS HELD EVERY year at the beginning of August. As the sailors raced, the town of Edgartown flung into action, with live music, sizzling burgers, craft beer, people milling about with vibrant smiles and glossy eyes and assured daydreams that summer perfection would last forever.

Still, as Christine and Lola stood near the starting line a bit before the race began, Christine felt a shift in the air. She felt an assurance that autumn would come swiftly, just after the stroke of September. It normally did, crushing all summer dreams and turning them to nostalgia.

"There he is," Lola said. She nodded toward Tommy Gasbarro, that hunk of a sailor, as he sauntered down the dock. His eyes lifted toward hers, and a sneaking smile spread between his cheeks.

Christine marveled at Lola's ability with men. She'd always had it.

"Did you already conduct the interview?" Christine asked as she sipped her sparkling wine.

"Yes. The article went up a few days ago. My editors loved it. They said Tommy looks like the perfect modern-day sailor," Lola said.

"Did you get more information about Stan?" Christine asked.

"Not really. Well, a bit," Lola said. "But we made plans to meet again."

Christine nudged her with her elbow. "That's my Lola."

Lola shrugged. "He seems fond of the old guy. Anyway, he's about to go on another pretty epic race, down to the Caribbean. I pitched the story about it to my editor and am waiting for feedback."

"Soon, he'll be all you cover, if you know what I mean," Christine countered.

Lola rolled her eyes. "I'm a professional," she said, unable to suppress a smile. "And I will do anything to get the best story."

Christine waved Charlotte, Rachel, and Claire over from the little pop-up bar, where Charlotte and Claire both grabbed glasses of sparkling rose. Susan had felt a bit too sick to attend the race. Amanda had already headed back to Newark, and Audrey had decided to slog around in her old t-shirt and read a book, citing that she already felt like a "pregnant cow" and didn't want to be seen in public. Of course, this was ridiculous. When they had said goodbye, Wes and Felix had been taking a nap together upstairs, a fact that made Christine smile even now. She loved that her family had adopted Felix as their own.

"And what is going on with you and Zach, anyway?" Lola said as the cousins lined up near the starting line.

Christine felt her cheeks burn red. "I mean, nothing, really," she answered, almost-honestly.

"Did you ever talk about why you hated each other?" Lola asked

"We did. It was a massive misunderstanding," Christine said.

"Of course it was," Lola said with a shrug. "Everyone always knew Zach had the hots for you."

"Whatever," Christine offered, although her heart felt warm.

They watched as the burly sailors, all seasoned and some Vineyard locals and others, tourists, along with several race-happy celebrities, boarded their sailboats and thrust their sails into the wind. The horn blared, and the race began with a chorus of Edgartown partiers cheering out over the Nantucket Sound.

When the last of the sailboats drifted out into the distance, Charlotte turned around and brightly said, "I guess it's time for some more drinks!" Together, the cousins and Rachel returned to the bar and hovered around other locals. Suddenly, the stage performer changed to reveal Zach, his guitar in-hand and his smile electric. From the crowd, Christine felt woozy as she clutched her sparkling wine. Zach strummed a few chords on the guitar and began to address the crowd.

"Hey there, everyone," he said. "Welcome to all of you. Vineyard residents, Edgartown locals, tourists—everyone is welcome here, especially on one of my favorite days of the year. The Round-the-Island Race. I have a few tunes to play for you today. This first one is about second chances."

Christine's heart hammered. Lola whispered, "I have a sneaking suspicion that I know who he's talking about."

Zach began to sing. Parts of the crowd quieted down to listen in, as Zach's voice swam through poetic verses. "You can't know how much I wish I'd known what we could have been."

"A little hammer on the nail, isn't it?" Lola continued in Christine's ear.

"Shhh," Christine whispered back. "I've never had a song written about me. I mean, not since that obsessive guy I dated in Brooklyn in my twenties."

"Ah! So many long lost stories you're keeping from me." Lola grinned.

After Zach's set, he joined Christine, Lola, and their cousins for a drink in the crowd. Another guitar was strummed in the distance, as Christine clutched Zach's elbow and said, "You really do amaze me, you know."

Zach's eyes glittered with happiness. "I could say the same for you. And for this food baby, I've almost constantly since you started baking at the bistro." He tapped his flat, muscular stomach as Christine rolled her eyes.

"Yeah, right," she scoffed.

The sky seemed to burn impossibly blue. As minutes ticked past, expectations for the race's end ramped up. Lola seemed like an anxious bird. Christine assumed it was all because she wanted Tommy Gasbarro to win the race.

"There he is," Lola said suddenly, gripping Christine's elbow so hard, she jumped.

Together, Lola and Christine stepped out toward the edge of the dock. Sure enough, Tommy Gasbarro swept toward the finish line, in first place, his black hair swirling in the wind. Lola looked captivated. The nearest boat in second place was at least fifty-yards behind; he seemed like the clear winner.

"This is going to make the story all the better," Lola whispered.

Suddenly, a gale wind rushed across the dock. It forced itself down on Christine's head, then swirled out across the water, thrusting itself against the large sail. Christine had gone sailing only a few times, but she knew, almost immediately, what would happen with his sail so full-flung, like it was now.

The boat tipped quickly. As it flung to the side, the boom smashed itself against Tommy Gasbarro's skull. Immediately, Tommy fell into the water, as the sailboat floated alongside him.

The crowd cried out, then grew hushed. Lola gripped Christine's hand hard like she had as a younger girl. Her eyes were like reflective pools.

"He's unconscious," Lola murmured, as Tommy floated face down.

"Oh my, God," Christine whispered.

A bright red medical boat motored toward Tommy's boat. Two lifeguards leaped into the water and propped Tommy up on red floaties, then delicately placed him on a floating stretcher. In all her years of living on the Vineyard, Christine had never seen anything like it.

"Oh, my God. Oh my, God," Lola said, over and over again. Her hand squeezed Christine's harder and harder.

As the lifeguards motored back to the dock, the first-place sailor surged over the finish line. Naturally, since he was meant to be second, nobody really clapped. The mood at the event had shifted considerably. Quickly, the lifeguards hustled down the dock, the stretcher lifted. When they reached the end, they slipped the stretcher delicately into an ambulance. Already, officials had cleared the sailboat from the race-arena, so that someone could prop it back up safely and return it to land. Everything had happened so quickly; it left Christine reeling.

When Christine turned around, she found Zach in a similar state of shock. "Did you recognize that guy?" he asked. "I think he won last year. Maybe even the year before."

"We kind of know him," Christine said. "Barely."

"I think we should go to the hospital," Lola blurted.

Zach looked incredulous. "Really? For someone you barely know?"

"He doesn't have people to check on him, really," Lola insisted. "Come on, Christine. Let's go."

Christine gave Zach a half-shrug, just as Lola yanked her through the crowd and snaked her back toward their car. When they reached it, Christine said, "I mean, he does have someone to check on him. And that's someone we might not want to run into today of all days?"

Lola seemed sure of herself, though, and not in the mood to argue. She snapped her seatbelt and frowned at Christine as she ambled into the passenger seat.

"Do you have to move so slowly?" she demanded.

They rocketed toward the hospital, with Lola cursing almost every passenger-crossing, every slow car. Her hands over the steering wheel were bright white. Admittedly, if something like this had happened to Zach, Christine might have reacted much the same way. It was still more proof that, as weird as it was, Lola had a pretty big thing for Stan Ellis's ex-step-son.

Hopefully, he would be all right.

They yanked into the emergency room parking lot. As they sprung out, Lola muttered, "I never thought I'd be spending so much time in hospitals." Christine didn't respond. They hustled toward the lobby of the emergency room, which was a flurry of activity. After all, the Edgartown Round-the-Island Race was one of the bigger parties of the year, which normally paved the way for several minor accidents. A teenager with a broken arm sat in the front line of chairs, trying not to cry. When Christine's eyes met his, he said, "I didn't even want to go skateboarding today." Beside him, his mother glowered and said, "I told you that thing would kill you."

Lola hustled up to the front desk and asked, "Was the sailor from the race already taken back?"

The woman blinked big, dull eyes at her and said, "What's his name?"

"Tommy. Tommy Gasbarro," Lola said.

The woman glanced at her notes and said, "There's really not a lot I can tell you right now. He's just arrived. In fact, you almost beat him here."

When Lola returned to Christine, she muttered under her breath. "They never know what they're doing at places like this."

"Yes, they do," Christine said. "Just give them a few minutes to figure it out."

Again, Lola muttered, but this time, too quietly for Christine to understand. She imagined the words were about her, anyway.

CHAPTER 23

CHRISTINE COAXED LOLA TOWARD THE BRIGHTER LINE OF chairs near the window. Lola clenched her hands over her knees and peered into space, while Christine headed toward the vending machines to buy two bottles of water and a bag of peanuts. They hadn't eaten properly that day, despite the insanely fatty, rich, and marvelous options at the street food fair in Edgartown. They would have to subsist on peanuts until Lola allowed them to leave; there was no telling when that would be.

When Christine returned to Lola, she dotted several peanuts out across Lola's palm and watched her chew slowly. When she swallowed, she muttered, "Thank you. I think I have low blood sugar. I just..." She closed her eyes tightly, then said, "When Tommy and I talked briefly about Stan, he said that he actually met Mom a few times. He's only a bit older than you, I guess, which means he would have been around Susan's age when Mom died."

Christine's heart hammered. She understood, more and more, why Lola had latched onto this guy and didn't want to let him go.

"We didn't get a chance to talk about it much," Lola continued. "He had to head off to visit Stan, and the news of it actually shocked me so much that I had to step away from it for a while and focus on the story for my editors. But gosh, Christine. Think about it. Our mom was so close with Stan Ellis that she actually met his ex-step-son, the person he felt closest to in his life. She had this whole other secret existence. And Stan and Tommy are the only two people on the planet who really know about it.

"But there's so much more to it, I'm sure," Lola added, taking a few more peanuts and speaking almost violently with her hands. "Regardless, Tommy saw Mom as a thirty-seven, thirty-eight-year-old woman. That's how old I am right now, before my birthday later this month. God. It's wild to think about it, isn't it?"

"Did he seem to know about the accident?" Christine asked in a hushed voice.

"Of course. Bits and pieces. He didn't go into it very much," Lola continued. "One thing he did mention was... Once, Stan and Dad got into some kind of fist-fight years ago, outside the Edgartown Bar. He had to make some kind of bail for Stan. Apparently, Tommy was the only person Stan could call."

Christine contemplated this for a long time. "Did he know about us? About Mom's daughters?"

"We didn't get that far." Lola bit hard on her lower lip. "Now that Audrey is about to be a mother, I'm thinking so much more about time, and how it all seems to slip through our fingers. I'm thinking about how we all get this particular perspective on everything that happened. And I..."

Christine felt a strange pang in her gut. Over the past few days, she had struggled with explaining to Lola the discussion between Audrey and herself. Audrey, whose mood had been lifted by the ordeal, had spent most of that time swimming and reading and avoiding her mother at all costs.

"We all have a very unique perspective," Christine echoed. Her eyes scanned the back of the emergency room as she drummed up the courage to say it. "Listen. Lola. I really am not sure how to say this to you."

"I just, I know Stan Ellis is evil. I know he's the enemy, and I know we have to talk to him about Mom at some point. I just have to think it's all a little more nuanced than that..." Lola continued.

"That isn't what I mean," Christine said. Her voice wavered so much it forced Lola's eyes toward her.

"What's going on?" Lola demanded.

Christine swallowed. How could she possibly describe all the thought that had gone into this decision? How could she make Lola feel as though she hadn't gone behind her back?

"More secrets, huh?" Lola said. "I don't know how much more of this I can take."

"It's just. Audrey and I had a conversation about the baby," Christine finally blurted out.

Lola crossed her arms tight over her chest. "And?"

"And we floated the idea that maybe, well. Maybe I could help raise the baby until she's ready to stand on her own two feet."

Lola's eyes became enormous. "Christine. You do know that Audrey is only nineteen, don't you?"

"Yes, of course. That's kind of the point," Christine returned.

"No. I mean. She only just left the house we shared together.

Every step of her first eighteen years, Audrey and I made decisions together. The two of us," Lola continued.

Christine's heart sank. "I understand."

"You can't just barrel into our relationship like this and start offering up big ideas," Lola said.

"You see how depressed she is about all this, don't you?" Christine demanded. "She misses her life. She wants the kind of career you want for her. She feels like she let you down. This is... I don't know. The perfect option?"

"That isn't for you to decide!" Lola cried. "Just because you're depressed doesn't mean everyone else is depressed."

Christine set her jaw. This last attack hurt the worst. "She just needs help," she muttered steadily. "If you'd just stop being so damn stubborn all the time, maybe you would understand it."

Suddenly, the automatic doors in the emergency room burst open. Stan Ellis surged into the lobby, his cheeks bright red. Sweat billowed down the back of his shirt and in his pits. The second he entered, he locked eyes with the Sheridan sisters.

He staggered to a halt. It was almost exactly like at the Edgartown Bar: all Stan Ellis wanted to do, at that moment, was get as far as he could away from Christine and Lola Sheridan.

Slowly, Lola and Christine got to their feet and walked toward him. Stan looked like a frozen deer in the center of the road, unsure of which direction to go. As they approached, the skateboarder kid with the busted arm howled with pain. It was a perfect soundtrack.

Stan spread his palms out in front of him and stepped back. This seemed almost comical like the Sheridan sisters had plans to eat him whole.

"Let's just have a little chat, Stan," Lola said.

"Nothing major," Christine said. "Just a casual catch-up between old friends."

"I didn't ask for any of this," Stan mumbled, hardly loud enough for them to hear.

"That's funny, Stan, because neither did we," Lola returned.

"I just want to check on Tommy," Stan blared.

"And you can. That's why we're all here," Lola said.

Stan's nostrils flared. As he walked backward, the doors sprung open behind him. With the sound of them opening, he tugged around and burst back into the summer air. Lola rushed toward the doors, but Christine reached out and grabbed her elbow.

"What are you doing?" Lola demanded. "He's getting away."

Christine's heart thudded. "His only family was just hurt badly in a sailing accident. I don't think right now is the perfect opportunity to do this."

Lola's eyes were fiery. She dropped her arms to her sides and nodded, although she looked on the verge of another angry outburst. Christine was reminded again that Lola had always been the sister who cried the most. Big, emotional highs and lows were her thing. This scene was another in a long story of Lola's life.

The receptionist stood from the desk and called Lola's name. "You said you were here for the sailor, didn't you?"

Lola hustled back to the counter and said, "Yes. Tommy Gasbarro."

"And you're family?" the woman asked.

"Yes," Lola returned. Immediately, she turned her head back to Christine, who gave her a crooked shrug.

Soon after, Lola disappeared between the double-wide emergency room doors. Christine hunkered in the corner for a while, staring at her toes. The conversation about Audrey's baby hadn't been fruitful, exactly, although she had to hope and pray that Lola would find the light in the tunnel eventually. Already, Christine's arms ached with hope for that baby. She wanted to carry her, to hold her against her, to sing songs to her when she couldn't sleep at night.

Already, she called the baby "she," as though she already knew the gender.

But how could the Sheridan sisters have anything else? Except Susan's Jake, of course. But he looked like Richard, through-and-through.

CHAPTER 24

It was just after four-thirty. Lola had been in the hospital room for over fifteen minutes, with no sign of reappearing. Christine's phone buzzed with a message from Zach.

ZACH WALTERS: Hey. How's it going at the hospital? I'm headed to the bistro. I think it's going to be extremely busy so soon after the race. If you're not busy with family stuff, would you mind stopping by? I need a competent head in there tonight.

Christine wrote to Lola that she was headed to the bistro. After all, she was no good to anyone in the emergency room lobby. She hustled up and grabbed a taxi out near the main entrance, which took her back to Oak Bluffs. When she reached the bistro, she found Zach in his office, tying a white apron around his trim waist.

"You called?" she said with a wide grin.

"My savior," he said.

They hovered there for a second, both of them analyzing the

other's face. Christine wanted to beg him to kiss her; maybe he wanted her to make a move. Still, after too much time had passed, Ronnie yanked the door open to make the announcement.

"We have a lot of drunk people out here, and they're all hungry!"

Christine and Zach burst into action, both probably a tiny bit grateful that neither of them had had to be brave. At least, that's how Christine felt about it. She scrubbed her hands while Ronnie had his seemingly-daily fake-panic, saying, "I just hope I can keep up with everything! It seems like it gets crazier every single day."

"You're a fantastic busboy, Ronnie," Christine returned. "Probably the best I've ever seen."

"You say that every day!"

"I know. And I mean it every day, too," she said with a grin.

One of the waiters called out that every table had been filled. Zach and Christine locked eyes. Baskets of in-house baked bread flew off the kitchen shelves and were placed on the center of each table, as a way to keep everyone calm. Their meals wouldn't take too long if everything went to plan, but anytime at all was a bit too long when it came to hungry drunk people.

Yet again, it seemed like they had never been stacked up like this at the bistro, but Christine had seen many nights just like that one at Chez Frank and she was always perfect under fire. She found herself giving orders and pep-talks, side-by-side, and flipping burgers, dressing plates, and firing crème brûlée on a constant rotation. She caught Zach watching her a few times, those blue beauties searing into her.

"Snap out of it!" she told him, giggling. "We need to focus."

"I can't," Zach whispered under his breath.

Just in the thick of the madness, Zach grabbed her hand and yanked her into the office again. He pressed her hard against the back of the door, just out of sight of everyone else in the kitchen, and kissed her like he meant it. When he lifted his head again, Christine's legs were jelly.

"Is that all you wanted to talk to me about?" she asked.

"I think that covers it," he returned.

Just like that, they were off again. They barreled back into the kitchen as though nothing had happened. Ronnie hustled into the kitchen with tear-stained cheeks and said, "A drunk woman spilled her drink on herself and blamed me!" And immediately, there were more fires to put out, more angry clients to assuage. Christine got lost in the chaos, falling into the hours until suddenly, she found herself leaning against the counter, panting, as the busboys cleaned up the last tables just after ten-thirty.

"Good job, everyone!" Zach called through the kitchen. He then opened the door out onto the war-zone of a dining area and said the same to the straggling wait staff and busboys out there. "Thank you for all you did today. Really spectacular stuff. I don't think we could have remained afloat without each and every one of you."

Christine and Zach helped for a bit with the clean-up, then removed their aprons and grabbed their things in the office. Zach snuck to the wine cellar to nab a bottle of French rose, and then he gripped Christine's hand and led her through the dining area and out onto the back porch, which looked out over the water. Christine heard several snickers from the wait staff as they walked hand-in-hand, along with several others, who whispered, "I knew it."

Still, she was bubbling over with happiness. As long as she

didn't focus on anything else and just on Zach, her stable rock, a foundation she had never known, which really made her feel so good. Really, really good.

They sat at the edge of the porch with their legs swinging down beneath them. Zach popped the wine cork and poured them both glasses. The moonlight shimmered perfectly over his face. With every second that passed, Christine swam in the memory of when Zach had grabbed her and pushed her against the door and made her forget her name.

"To a wonderful night," Zach said, clinking his glass with hers. "Thank you again for coming."

"Of course."

"What happened at the hospital?"

Christine heaved a sigh. Although she'd touched on it very briefly during their sleepover the previous week, she went into more detail about Stan Ellis, her mother, and Stan Ellis's new ex-step-son, who they hadn't known anything about.

"Lola seems smitten with him," Christine continued. "But while we waited for him in the lobby, Stan Ellis arrived. We had a stand-off and then he just ran away. Like he did at..."

"Ah! That's right," Zach said, snapping his fingers. "I understand, now. That night at Edgartown Bar."

"I'm afraid so," Christine said.

"He's your elusive ghost," Zach returned.

"Yes. I suppose so and we're his too." Christine swallowed. Slowly, she inched her hand across Zach's knee. Somehow, she wanted to touch him in as many ways as she could. She'd never wanted someone so badly before; it felt like an animal, eating her up from the inside.

"Zach. I feel like I should say something."

Zach's eyes burned toward her. "What's up?"

"I've been afraid of intimacy and honesty for basically my entire life," Christine continued. "I don't even know if I could be honest with my sisters or my mother when it mattered the most. Right now, now that I've lost so much, I want to try my best to be as honest with you as I can at every single juncture.

"I also want to be brave enough to demand what I want in this life. I think part of the reason I've been so lost is that I haven't really known what I wanted. I was overly willing to get too drunk to think about it. That's how I've lived the past twenty years of my life.

"But I'm done with that, now. I want to start something new, and I want to start it with you. You should know, though, that there is a more than likely possibility that I will be raising my niece's baby, at least until she's ready to take the reins. She's only nineteen years old, and the thought of struggling through that life right now terrifies her. Lucky for her, the thought of it thrills me. The first smile. The first steps. The little hugs and the laughter. Even the diaper changes. Everything about it."

Christine squeezed her eyes shut, trying to force herself not to hope too much.

Zach's hands found hers and held them tightly. His thumb traced across the top of her knuckles. When she opened her eyes again, she found him sharing the slightest smile with her.

"You look so beautiful right now," he marveled.

"I'm not used to being so honest."

"It suits you," Zach said. "And you know what else suits you? This version of motherhood. Although..." He gave a slight shrug. "I don't know if there's any reason we can't adopt more—down the line, I mean."

Christine looked at him in shock. She could feel the tears starting but held them back and threw her arms around him instead. She held him tightly against her. She wasn't sure whether to laugh or just cry. When she fell back, Zach wiped the tears that she couldn't hold back anymore from her cheeks. His smile was infectious.

"I can't believe I get another chance at life with my mortal high school enemy," he said chuckling.

"If you had told me even two months ago that I might be falling in love with Zach Walters from Martha's Vineyard, I would have smacked you across the face," Christine returned.

Christine held her head tighter against his chest and gazed out across the waves. Zach's heartbeat was sure, solid: the kind of sound that she could rely on. She imagined them several years from now, with Audrey's baby, aged three, and maybe another adopted baby, one she would be allowed to call her own forever.

Her heart hurt at the enormity of all of it. She ached that her mother was long gone and would never know Audrey or Amanda, her grandchildren; she hated that Zach had already been through so many horrors with the death of his own girl, Quinn.

But Christine knew that you had to press forward. You have to fight for the life you want, armed with the love of the ones who know you best. And there was no better place on earth to do that than on Martha's Vineyard.

CHAPTER 25

CHRISTINE SPENT THE NIGHT AT ZACH'S PLACE. WHEN HE dropped her off the following morning, she found Audrey and Amanda on the back porch, in front of another selection of wedding magazines. Nobody had mentioned that Amanda would be returning, but the sight of the two cousins together again filled her heart.

"And where on earth have you been, young lady?" Audrey said, arching her brow.

Christine laughed as the girls put on a little show for her: crossing their arms and pretending to be her parents.

"We were worried sick when you didn't come home last night," Amanda boomed, pretending to be the father.

"All night, we stayed up watching the window and wondering. And you know what I keep asking myself, Amanda?"

"What's that, Audrey?"

"I keep asking myself, what did we do so wrong to lead her so astray?" Audrey continued with a straight face.

Lola appeared at the porch steps and burst into laughter. "Are they doing their routine?"

"Oh, yeah. They're giving me the full brunt of it and they are damn good," Christine said.

Lola headed up the steps, wearing only a bikini, her hair drenched from a swim. She grabbed a hanging towel and wrapped it around herself.

"I can't believe my mom is going to have better abs than me soon," Audrey grumbled.

"Your body is going to pop back like that," Lola said, snapping her fingers. She turned her eyes back toward Christine and said, "By the way. We talked about it and... You and Audrey are right. It is the best idea. Thank you so much for offering. I can't think of a better person to take the reins of my grandbaby until she's ready to do it."

Christine hugged Lola a bit too hard so that a lot of her shirt was drenched in seawater. When she stepped back, laughing, her eyes met with Susan's. Susan also stood at the base of the steps, and in her hand, she held an electric razor. Her eyes meant business.

All the Sheridan women stared down at Susan. Susan lifted the razor higher and said, her voice booming, "It's time."

Nobody spoke for a long time. Finally, Amanda said, "Mom. Are you sure you want to do this?"

"Isn't it better to just get it over with?" Susan asked. She marched up the steps and gingerly knelt toward the outdoor electrical outlet, where she plugged it in. "And I want you girls to do it. I want it to be a little party—just the five of us."

Lola shrugged, entered the house, and came back with a pair of shears. "I checked on Dad. He's upstairs asleep with Felix again. I swear that cat calms him down so much."

"He did the same for me all these years," Christine admitted.

Audrey fetched the radio from inside and changed it to the '90s station. Susan clapped her hands and said, "Oh, I love this song," as Natalie Imbruglia's "Torn" churned in from the airwaves. "It's the perfect one to play while you snip my hair away. Who wants to do the first honors?"

Lola placed the scissors in Amanda's outstretched palm. "I'll do it, Mom, but only because you want me to," Amanda said.

"That's my girl. Thank you," Susan said.

Amanda brought a long piece of Susan's glorious dark hair skyward and grimaced. "Should we say something before I start cutting?"

"Susan, you always had the prettiest hair," Lola said with a sigh.

"It looks just like yours, Lola. We all have the same, dark, chestnut hair. Finally, I'll differentiate myself from you two," Susan said, chuckling. "Good riddance, I think. I spent way too much time with a flat iron all these years."

"All right. Count of three," Amanda said.

Together, the Sheridan women recited, "One, two, three," and Amanda cut the first long wedge of hair. It fluttered to the porch ground, and Amanda blinked at it for a long time.

"See?" Susan said in the silence. "It doesn't hurt at all."

They got to work after that. Amanda did several more pieces, before handing off the scissors to Lola and Christine and Audrey. Everyone had a turn until finally, Lola got impatient and cut off the rest. Then, she took the electric razor and buzzed it close around Susan's head, making perfect, lawnmower lines.

"Wow," Christine breathed. She felt she had never seen anything braver.

"Finally," Susan said. She snapped her palms together and stood again. She seemed to have more energy than usual, probably because it had been a few days since her last chemo treatment. "Now, I should tell you, everyone is coming over for a BBQ at noon."

"Everyone?" Lola groaned.

"Yes. Everyone," Susan said. "We haven't had a proper party here in a few weeks, and I don't want the summer to go to waste. This means that we all have quite a few jobs to do to get this place ready in time. I have Scott out now buying bags of ice, but that leaves us to buy burger meat, chips, pop, and some beer and wine. I've made a list." She grabbed a piece of paper from her back pocket and unfurled it.

"Ugh. Susan Sheridan, off to the races again," Lola said with a sneaky grin.

"Don't be sassy, Lorraine," Susan returned. "Oh, and Christine. I should tell you. Whoever it was you were with last night, I want you to invite him. This is a family affair, and everyone knows you're falling in love with someone. I've just been too out of it to find out who it is. Give us all a break and just include him in the family already."

With that, Susan burst back into the house, leaving a pile of her long-dead and already forgotten hair on the ground behind her.

Lola clucked her tongue and said, "I really never know what any of us are going to do next."

Christine still glowed after the night she'd had with Zach. Grateful she had the day off from the bistro, she flung into action to help Susan prepare another of her terrific BBQs at the house. She leaped back into the car to drive Lola and Amanda to the little grocery store at the edge of downtown, where they piled two carts with beer, wine, burgers and chips and countless other little snacks, including hummus, which Amanda insisted on. "We've got a health nut over here," Lola said with a smile as Amanda slipped the hummus into the cart.

"Hey. Only one of us has to wear a wedding dress," Amanda said.

"Don't speak so soon. Both Christine and I are hunting for our grooms, too." Lola winked.

Amanda laughed. "Fair enough. Maybe we'll have a whole year of weddings."

"On second thought, maybe we should get more hummus," Christine offered teasingly.

Back at the house, they piled up the snacks and fired up the grill. Scott arrived, carrying large bags of ice from his truck to the cooler. He stopped short when he saw Susan for the first time, but there was no less love in his eyes. He stepped up the porch steps and gazed at her, mesmerized, then placed his hands on her cheeks and whispered, "You're the most beautiful woman in the world." He kissed her in front of everyone.

When their kiss broke, Susan looked a tiny bit woozy, but she soon smiled and said, "And you're the most amazing man ever! But are you sure this is enough ice?"

Everyone laughed and said that he'd certainly brought enough. This was a constant worry at every BBQ, one that seemed to put any BBQ organizer in a tizzy. Christine wondered if she and Zach would ever have a BBQ for family and friends in Edgartown, if she ended up moving in with him, that is. These were early days; words could very well be empty promises.

Of course, she really didn't think they were.

Just after one, Wes awoke from his nap and padded down the steps with Felix hot on his heels. He stepped out onto the porch to find the beginnings of a BBQ, and he chortled with laughter.

"I have to say. This loss of memory stuff really makes for some unique surprises," he said.

"Don't worry, Dad. This was a surprise to all of us, too," Christine offered.

"My, my. Susan," Wes said. His grin broadened when he spotted her. "It looks good."

Susan patted her head absentmindedly. "Oh, sure. It doesn't matter to me much. Do you think you could change into something a little more formal? It's just, everyone is coming over, and I don't think they necessarily want to see you in your sleeping shirt."

Audrey hopped up in her sleeping shirt and stretched it out in front of her. This particular one was covered in Snoopy designs. "Does that go for me, too, Aunt Susie?"

"Absolutely," Susan said. "Everyone, let's try to put our best foot forward. We're the Sheridan clan, and we're here to stay."

People started to arrive just after one. Naturally, Aunt Kerry and Uncle Trevor arrived first, carting their twin grandchildren, Abby and Gail, along with them. Soon after, Claire and her husband, Russel, arrived, with Claire chasing Gail down to give her allergy medicine. After that, came Charlotte and Rachel, Kelli and her husband, Mike, along with their children, Sam, Josh, and Lexi.

After that, non-family members, who might as well have been family members, arrived, including Lily and Sarah, Susan's best friends from high school. Both of them squeezed Christine tight.

"I had no idea you were going to stay, Christine!" Lily cried. "Susan had told me you'd gone back to New York City, and I just never envisioned the likes of you returning. But then, one day, my husband Timothy came back to the house with these remarkable croissants. I couldn't shut up about these croissants, I'm telling you. I come to find out you're the one who baked them!"

"Guilty." Christine grinned. In her brooding, teenage years, she'd never particularly liked Susan's friends. Now, she couldn't remember why.

"Are more people talking about the croissants?" Zach's voice boomed from behind her, forcing her to turn quickly and fall into a hug.

"I didn't think you could get away from the bistro so soon," Christine murmured into his ear.

His hand found the little curve of her lower back. "Who could turn down a classic Sheridan family BBQ? I heard they're the best parties on the island."

Susan returned from the kitchen with her hands on her hips. She'd changed into a dynamite purple dress, which highlighted her powerful curves and her flat waist. Her eyes burned toward Zach as she said, "Ah! I guess I should have known. Zach Walters, good to have you here."

"Thanks for having me, Susan," Zach said. Then, he turned and whispered to Christine, "What is she talking about?"

"She knew I was falling for someone, but she didn't know who," Christine returned.

The party was off to the races. Scott had long since started piling burgers and hot dogs onto people's plates, and various members of the clan sat at the extra picnic tables in the yard that led down toward the Sound. As Christine and Zach walked toward the long table, where they'd placed out bottles of wine, Aunt Kerry gripped her elbow and yanked her back.

"Are you going to introduce me to your handsome young man?" she demanded.

Christine chuckled. "I thought maybe you'd met? He's the head chef at the bistro at the Inn."

Aunt Kerry's lips turned to a round O. "My goodness, young man. You're doing a remarkable job over there, you know. Really wonderful."

"Thank you. I couldn't have done it without Christine. She's changed the place around since she came back to the island," he said.

Wes, who sat across from Aunt Kerry, beamed at them. "You two make a great couple," he said. "I love seeing my Christine this happy."

Christine blushed, while Zach made small talk with Wes about the Inn and the bistro. Although Wes didn't work there so often anymore, he still wanted to feel informed about every aspect.

When Christine headed toward the grill to grab a burger for herself, Susan drew her toward the side of the porch and said, "It's so funny, isn't it? I mean, I never would have imagined the two of us to take over what our parents did. Now, you and Zach will run the bistro, and Scott and I will run the Inn... it's perfect."

"It really is," Christine agreed.

Susan's bottom lip bounced for a moment, the only sign the

entire day that any of this had been hard for her. "Honestly, if I didn't have my sisters with me during this time, I don't know what I would do. It was one of the first thoughts I had when I got my very first diagnosis. I just wanted you girls close."

Christine's eyes filled with tears. She hugged Susan, swallowing a lump in her throat, and murmured, "But you're going to be okay. Right?"

"The doctor says my odds are fantastic," Susan said, breaking the hug. "I am the luckiest bald woman in the world. I don't feel crazy saying that, either."

"Did you ever tell Richard about it?" Christine asked.

Susan shrugged. "I think the kids did. I got a message from him the other day asking if I 'needed anything.' I wanted to say something snarky back about how he'd never given me anything I needed, but I held back."

Christine and Zach found space at one of the further picnic tables, toward the water. Zach had piled his burger outrageously high: with pickles and smears of mustard and vibrant purple onions.

"It's not haute cuisine, but it is delicious," he said. "In the sloppiest way, imaginable."

"Your chin looks like a Van Gogh painting." Christine laughed.

Audrey appeared on the other side of the table as Christine smeared a napkin across Zach's chin. She clucked her tongue and placed backhands over her stomach. Naturally, it was still normal stomach size, with zero indication of the soon to be baby.

"Well, well. If it isn't the future long-term babysitters of my child," Audrey said.

Zach lifted his eyebrows. "Ah! So you're the one."

"Yes. I suppose I'm pretty famous around here," Audrey replied. She slipped onto the bench across from them, placing a plate of what looked to be exclusively different kinds of potato chips on the table in front of her.

Christine made a mental note to talk to her about pregnancy nutrition. Now wasn't the time, though.

"Should there be some kind of interview or something?" Zach said chuckling.

"Hmm." Audrey placed a chip between her teeth and chewed the very edge. "That's a great idea. Trying to think of a good question. Okay. Let's say my baby is crying in the middle of the night. What song do you sing her to get her to fall asleep?"

"The baby is a she?" Zach asked.

"Just answer the question," Audrey returned.

"Okay. It seems like a tough one." Zach rubbed his palms together, imitating intense concentration, and said, "Okay. How about... Um. Taylor Swift?"

"Ding! I will accept this answer," Audrey said. "As long as it's her earlier stuff. Anything else gets a little too angry for late-night sleeping babies."

Christine laughed as Zach snaked his arm over her shoulders, hugged her tight, and said, "Look, babe! We're doing it! We're passing the test!"

"Okay, okay. Here's another one," Audrey continued. "Will you let me come see her whenever I want to? And can I stay with you?"

"Of course," Christine said. "Wherever we are, you are welcome at any time. You're the baby's mother."

"Right. I'm her mother," Audrey said.

"Again, very confused about how you know the gender already," Zach said.

"Women's intuition, of course," Audrey said with a shrug.

The afternoon flooded into the evening. Christine and Zach and Audrey laughed together for plenty of it, with Audrey finding new "difficult" parent questions to ask them. Several times, Zach brought up the idea of adoption, at which Audrey screamed with excitement. Of course, to downplay that joy, she said, "But you'll, of course, treat my girl as your favorite."

"No favorites!" Zach said.

"Ugh. Fine," Audrey laughed.

Christine had never felt so free in her life. As the night closed down around them, she placed her head on Zach's shoulder and gazed out at the water. Fireflies danced through the night air, buzzing out their vibrant light and then whipping it back into their bodies. Like a child whom, generally speaking, she still was, and was still allowed to be—Audrey drew out her palms and cupped a firefly between them. She then drew it back, holding it so that her cupped hands became a lantern. She whispered something into her hands and then opened them apart so that the firefly flew away, free to cast its light across the night once more.

"What did you say?" Christine asked.

Audrey pressed her finger against her lips. "I wished for something. I can't tell you what it is, or it might not come true."

"Gosh, I missed these firefly nights," Lola said, coming up from behind with a glass of wine in her hand. "It's truly the most magical place on earth."

Nobody spoke for a long time. All Christine could hear was the strong thud of Zach's heart as she pressed herself against him: her rock, her love, the answer to her dreams. She clenched her eyes and cast a wish to all the fireflies.

Don't let us lose each other again. Let us have eight thousand more nights, just like this.

You can pre-order August Sunsets Book Three everywhere!
August Sunsets on Amazon
https://books2read.com/u/boEWav

CONNECT WITH KATIE WINTERS

Facebook
Amazon
Goodreads
Bookbub

Made in United States
North Haven, CT
01 February 2023

31918513R00136